T. M. A

ONE MAN, ONE MATCHET

HEB

HEINEMANN

LONDON IBADAN NAIROBI

Heinemann Educational Books Ltd
48 Charles Street, London W1X 8AH
P.M.B. 5205, Ibadan · P.O. Box 45314, Nairobi ·
P.O. Box 3966, Lusaka
EDINBURGH MELBOURNE TORONTO AUCKLAND
SINGAPORE HONG KONG KUALA LUMPUR NEW DELHI

ISBN 0 435 90011 0

First published 1964
First published in *African Writers Series* 1965
Reprinted 1966, 1968, 1969, 1970, 1972, 1974

Printed in Malta by
St Paul's Press Ltd

AFRICAN WRITERS SERIES LIST

Founding editor · Chinua Achebe

Keys to Signs

Novels are unmarked
*Short Stories
†Poetry
‡Plays
§Autobiography or Biography

PETER ABRAHAMS
6 *Mine Boy*

CHINUA ACHEBE
1 *Things Fall Apart*
3 *No Longer at Ease*
16 *Arrow of God*
31 *A Man of the People*
100 *Girls at War**
120 *Beware Soul Brother*†

TEWFIK AL-HAKIM
117 *Fate of a Cockroach*‡

T. M. ALUKO
11 *One Man, One Matchet*
30 *One Man, One Wife*
32 *Kinsman and Foreman*
70 *Chief, the Honourable Minister*
130 *His Worshipful Majesty*

ELECHI AMADI
25 *The Concubine*
44 *The Great Ponds*
140 *Sunset in Biafra*§

JARED ANGIRA
111 *Silent Voices*†

I. N. C. ANIEBO
148 *The Anonymity of Sacrifice*

AYI KWEI ARMAH
43 *The Beautyful Ones Are Not Yet Born*

BEDIAKO ASARE
59 *Rebel*

KOFI AWOONOR
108 *This Earth, My Brother*

FRANCIS BEBEY
86 *Agatha Moudio's Son*

MONGO BETI
13 *Mission to Kala*
77 *King Lazarus*
88 *The Poor Christ of Bomba*

OKOT p'BITEK
147 *The Horn of My Love*†

DENNIS BRUTUS
46 *Letters to Martha*†
115 *A Simple Lust*†

SYL CHENEY-COKER
126 *Concerto for an Exile*†

DRISS CHRAIBI
79 *Heirs to the Past*

J. P. CLARK
50 *America, Their America*§

WILLIAM CONTON
12 *The African*

BERNARD B. DADIÉ
87 *Climbié*

DANIACHEW
125 *The Thirteenth Sun*

MODIKWE DIKOBE
124 *The Marabi Dance*

MBELLA SONNE DIPOKO
57 *Because of Women*
82 *A Few Nights and Days*
107 *Black and White in Love*†

AMU DJOLETO
41 The Strange Man

CYPRIAN EKWENSI
2 *Burning Grass*
5 *People of the City*
19 *Lokotown**
84 *Beautiful Feathers*
146 *Jagua Nana*

OLAUDAH EQUIANO
10 *Equiano's Travels*§

MALICK FALL
144 *The Wound*

NURUDDIN FARAH
80 *From a Crooked Rib*

MUGO GATHERU
20 *Child of Two Worlds*

BESSIE HEAD
101 *Maru*
149 *A Question of Power*

LUIS BERNARDO HONWANA
60 *We Killed Mangy-Dog**

SONALLAH IBRAHIM
95 *The Smell of It**

OBOTUNDE IJIMERE
18 *The Imprisonment of Obatala*‡

AUBREY KACHINGWE
24 *No Easy Task*

CHEIKH HAMIDOU KANE
119 *Ambiguous Adventure*

KENNETH KAUNDA
4 *Zambia Shall Be Free*§

ASARE KONADU
40 *A Woman in her Prime*
55 *Ordained by the Oracle*

DURO LADIPO
65 *Three Yoruba Plays*‡

ALEX LA GUMA
35 *A Walk in the Night**
110 *In the Fog of the Seasons' End*
152 *The Stone Country*

DORIS LESSING
131 *The Grass is Singing*

TABAN LO LIYONG
69 *Fixions**
74 *Eating Chiefs**
90 *Frantz Fanon's Uneven Ribs*†
116 *Another Nigger Dead*†

BONNIE LUBEGA
105 *The Outcasts*

YULISA AMADU MADDY
89 *Obasai*‡
137 *No Past, No Present, No Future*

NAGUIB MAHFOUZ
151 *Midaq Alley*

NELSON MANDELA
123 *No Easy Walk to Freedom*§

RENÉ MARAN
135 *Batouala*

ALI A. MAZRUI
97 *The Trial of Christopher Okigbo*

TOM MBOYA
81 *The Challenge of Nationhood*§

S. O. MEZU
113 *Behind the Rising Sun*

HAM MUKASA
133 *Apolo Kagwa Discovers Britain*

DOMINIC MULAISHO
98 *The Tongue of the Dumb*

JOHN MUNONYE
21 *The Only Son*
45 *Obi*
94 *Oil Man of Obange*
121 *A Wreath for the Maidens*

MEJA MWANGI
143 *Kill Me Quick*
145 *Carcase for Hounds*

NGUGI WA THIONG'O
7 *Weep Not Child*
17 *The River Between*
36 *A Grain of Wheat*
51 *The Black Hermit‡*
150 *Secret Lives**

ARTHUR NORTJE
141 *Dead Roots†*

NKEM NWANKWO
67 *Danda*

FLORA NWAPA
26 *Efuru*
56 *Idu*

ONUORA NZEKWU
85 *Wand of Noble Wood*
91 *Blade Among the Boys*

OGINGA ODINGA
38 *Not Yet Uhuru§*

GABRIEL OKARA
68 *The Voice*

CHRISTOPHER OKIGBO
62 *Labyrinths†*

KOLE OMOTOSO
102 *The Edifice*
122 *The Combat*

SEMBENE OUSMANE
63 *God's Bits of Wood*
92 *The Money-Order with White Genesis*
142 *Tribal Scars**

YAMBO OUOLOGUEM
99 *Bound to Violence*

MARTIN OWUSU
138 *The Sudden Return‡*

FERDINAND OYONO
29 *Houseboy*
39 *The Old Man and the Medal*

PETER K. PALANGYO
53 *Dying in the Sun*

LENRIE PETERS
22 *The Second Round*
37 *Satellites†*
103 *Katchikali†*

MWANGI RUHENI
139 *The Future Leaders*

TAYEB SALIH
47 *The Wedding of Zein**
66 *Season of Migration to the North*

STANLAKE SAMKANGE
33 *On Trial for my Country*

KOBINA SEKYI
136 *The Blinkards‡*

SAHLE SELLASSIE
52 *The Afersata*

FRANCIS SELORMEY
27 *The Narrow Path*

L. S. SENGHOR
71 *Nocturnes†*

ROBERT SERUMAGA
54 *Return to the Shadows*

WOLE SOYINKA
76 *The Interpreters*

TCHICAYA U TAM'SI
72 *Selected Poems†*

CAN THEMBA
104 *The Will to Die**

REMS NNA UMEASIEGBU
61 *The Way We Lived**

LAWRENCE VAMBE
112 *An Ill-Fated People§*

D. M. ZWELONKE
128 *Robben Island*

COLLECTIONS OF STORIES AND PROSE
9 *Modern African Prose* Edited by Richard Rive
114 *Quartet* By Richard Rive, Alex La Guma, Alf Wannenburgh and James Matthews
15 *Origin East Africa* Edited by David Cook
23 *The Origin of Life and Death* Edited by Ulli Beier
48 *Not Even God is Ripe Enough* Edited by Bakare Gbadamosi and Ulli Beier
58 *Political Spider* Edited by Ulli Beier
73 *North African Writing* Translated by Len Ortzèn
75 *Myths and Legends of the Swahili* Edited by Jan Knappert
83 *Myths and Legends of the Congo* Edited by Jan Knappert
109 *Onitsha Market Literature* Edited by E. N. Obiechina
118 *Amadu's Bundle* Malum Amadu Edited by Gulla Kell and Ronald Moody
132 *Two Centuries of African English* Edited by Lalage Bown

ANTHOLOGIES OF POETRY
8 *A Book of African Verse* Edited by John Reed and Clive Wake
42 *Poems from Ghana* Edited by Kofi Awoonor and G. Adali-Mortty
64 *Seven South African Poets* Edited by Cosmo Pieterse
93 *A Choice of Flowers* Translated by Jan Knappert
96 *Poems from East Africa* Edited by David Cook and David Rubadiri
106 *French African Verse* Translated by John Reed and Clive Wake
129 *Igbo Traditional Verse* Edited by Romanus Egudu and Donatus Nwoga

COLLECTIONS OF PLAYS
28 *Short East African Plays* Edited by David Cook and David Rubadiri
34 *Ten One-Act Plays* Edited by Cosmo Pieterse
78 *Short African Plays* Edited by Cosmo Pieterse
114 *Five African Plays* Edited by Cosmo Pieterse
127 *Nine African Plays for Radio* Edited by Cosmo Pieterse and Gwyneth Henderson
134 *African Theatre* Edited by Gwyneth Henderson

To my daughter Toyin
and her little brothers

CHAPTER ONE

Cocoa disease – the new threat to the prosperity of the farmers and to the premier industry of the nation. This, said the white District Officer, was the main business of the meeting. He stood there in his limp khaki while beside him the Council Clerk translated into the vernacular. So important was the problem, he explained, that the Agricultural Officer himself had come all the way from Headquarters to address the farmers. He hoped they would pay attention to all the things he had to tell them and later on to the things that Chief Joseph Ajayi, their own representative, would say.

Farmers' representatives and village heads settled themselves on wooden benches as the District Officer sat down. He looked exhausted. The Court House was packed to capacity, and the still humid air and inadequate ventilation made the place thoroughly uncomfortable for the Englishman.

The Agricultural Officer rose to speak. He said that he was not happy to be among them. He said he wished he could pretend to be, but he was not. For the situation that occasioned his visit was very grave indeed. So grave that the Government had diverted vast sums of money originally meant for other projects to the combating of the disease. Government had sent two specialists to the Tropical Agriculture Research Institute, far far away in the West Indies, to study the cause and the cure of the disease. All indication was to the effect that there was no known cure. Prevention was the only cure, he emphasized. For this reason Government had sent a special team of cocoa disease workers and representatives of farmers' cooperative unions to the neighbouring country where the disease had caused widespread devastation and, but for the timely action of their Government, would have brought certain ruin to its major industry. He was glad that their own representative, an Ipaja man like themselves, was present that morning and would tell them what he had seen.

'This country is essentially agricultural, and will always be agricultural.' The civil servant repeated the age-worn yardstick of government policy. 'And upon you farmers depends the future of your country.' He paused while the Clerk translated. A small, bald-headed man nodded approvingly at the compliment. But Chief Momo sat unmoved.

'Government's effort, however, amounts to nothing without your cooperation,' the Agricultural Officer continued. Again the small man hailed the announcement with a nod. He beamed happily round the assembly from his own bench. Government was at last recognizing the indispensability of the farmer. Government was at last placing emphasis where it should be placed. Still Chief Momo sat unimpressed. He was not going to commit himself until he knew where the Agricultural Officer's speech was leading. He was too old a fish to be caught in the White Man's net of sweet words.

'And trusting to that cooperation,' the Agricultural Officer was concluding, 'I hope you will all listen attentively to what Chief Joseph Ajayi has to tell you. I would like to say here that he was a very popular member of the team that went on the tour. Both we and our hosts were very fond of him. I think he is a most delightful person, a representative that any group of people should be proud of any day. And after he has finished speaking to you, I hope you will watch carefully the lantern slides I shall show you. There you will see how your brother farmers in the neighbouring territory are fighting the disease.'

Chief Joseph Ajayi strode to the front. He was a giant of a man. He adjusted the ample sleeves of his big *agbada* on his heavy shoulders and bellowed out greetings lavishly in characteristic Yoruba fashion. He was happy to be back among them, his own friends and people. Not that he was not happy among their brother farmers who were their hosts where they went. Indeed he and his party were very well entertained, and he would testify any day to the large-scale hospitality they received. Farmers were farmers anywhere in the world as far as offering to fellow farmers food from the produce of mother earth was concerned.

He spoke of the voyage, and dwelt a little on the might of God and the cleverness of the White Man in making mere water carry the mighty boat in which he and his party had travelled.

He described in vivid detail the widespread devastation the disease had caused on the farms he and his party had visited. Whole plantations of cocoa trees devoid of leaves. Trees with young cocoa pods that turned brown and withered away before reaching maturity. Trees on which the very few pods that did grow big turned black with disease. It was terrible, he said, and sad. He shuddered at the recollection of the terrible things he had seen.

Once a tree was attacked by the disease it was a dead tree, he explained in grave emphasis. And from tree to tree the disease spread until it was eventually relayed round the entire plantation. The most disturbing aspect of the whole situation was that there was no known cure for the disease. If there were, the White Man would have found it and given it to them. They all knew how clever the White Man was in everything.

Then he took a deep breath, to indicate the importance of the news to come, and announced importantly to his listeners that the one and only cure was to cut down all trees in which symptoms of the disease had appeared.

Ugly frowns met the ugly announcement after its meaning had sunk in. Men hissed and looked round at one another. They grumbled and murmured and chattered amongst themselves.

'That we should cut down cocoa trees – the tree of all

wealth!' the small, bald-headed man piped diffidently. He looked scared and disillusioned. He gaped round the group, astonished at hearing such sacrilege against the tree that to him was the god of all wealth.

Chief Momo sighed, and shook his head. He had at no time expected anything sane from the White Man, and was therefore not surprised at this outrageous suggestion. He collected his umbrella and his cap from under the bench, angrily wiped the dust from them, and rose to depart. He had no time for men who talked such lunacy.

But half-way across the hall he stopped abruptly. He wheeled round, and glared at the unfortunate Chief Ajayi with an evil eye. 'Ajayi,' he cried out. 'It is you I wish to speak to. I do not wish to speak to that White Man sitting behind you. Why, he calls himself a farmer – a farmer indeed, with hands too soft to hold a hoe without blistering; a farmer, with back too stiff to bend on the farm; a farmer with feet too tender to walk without shoes.'

He paused, and the atmosphere grew more tense.

'He is not one of us. He does not understand the hardships we suffer when we tend our cocoa trees from seedlings to maturity. He does not know how much sweat we have to wipe from our faces when we work under the sun; he does not know how many insects have bitten us, how many thorns have cut our feet. If it is that he knew these things he would not have said that we should with our own hands cut down our own cocoa trees. Must we wait for him to tell us to begin to cut off each other's heads before we know that he truly wants to destroy us? We already know that he does not like us. He does not like our town – we know that he likes Apeno, not Ipaja.'

His eyes swept round the assembly. Nods everywhere approved his words. Then he continued: 'When they asked us to come to this meeting, we thought they probably had something good to tell us. We thought that they would perhaps pay us more money for our cocoa because they saw how very much we were suffering. We thought perhaps they would pity us and tell us not to pay taxes any more. Are these not the things we have been asking for all this time? But what do we get instead?' Again his gaze left the platform for a moment and swept round the assembly. 'We must cut down our cocoa trees. And why must we cut down our cocoa trees? They say we must cut them down because they are ill. Ha, ha, ha!' He laughed in derision. 'Cocoa trees are ill, do you all hear that? Do you all hear that trees are ill? Does disease not make man himself go ill? Does death not kill man himself? And does disease not catch the White Man himself? And did a white man not die the other day – was his brother the white doctor able to save him? No one was able to save him because that day on which he died was his appointed day to go back to the Land of the Dead. Before he was conceived and born by his mother did he not promise the gods that he would return to them that day? Can anyone change that appointed day? They say that the White Man knows everything. Yes, he knows everything. But can the White Man himself in all his knowledge change the appointed day? If therefore we cannot prevent a man from dying why should we worry so much because a tree is dying? If one dies, can we not plant a seed from which another will grow? And you, Chief, you, you Joseph Ajayi,' he pointed his umbrella menacingly, 'you who are one of us, you who eat the oil from the palm fruits of the land, you who drink the water of Agbara stream like us – you, Joseph Ajayi, son of our land, and a chief of our town, you join in this mad conspiracy against your own kin – you – you – you —'

Speechless with rage, he turned and walked out of the meeting.

Neither the District Officer nor the Agricultural Officer understood what Chief Momo had said. He had spoken his own dialect of Yoruba in which the older civil servant had passed the first prescribed examination. But this qualification was completely inadequate for understanding an angry farmer speaking not the standard Yoruba accepted by Government but the sing-song of the Ipaja dialect. There was, however, no mistaking the meaning of the menacing gestures with the umbrella.

The Clerk's powerful voice rose above the ensuing pandemonium. He clapped his hands and cried for order several times. The District Officer's orderly blew his whistle and eventually order of some sort was restored.

The Clerk then pleaded with the people. Such behaviour, he explained, was unbecoming of such an assembly of chiefs, elders and society leaders. It undermined their national dignity, and lowered their standing in the eye of the White Man. If they did not like the idea of cutting out their cocoa trees, he himself could not blame them. But a more fitting course of action would be to tell the District Officer and the Agricultural Officer that they required some time to consider the weighty problem and that they would bring their answer to him some other day. That answer would not commit them in any way whatsoever. That was what was known as diplomacy in international politics. They should all remember the various schemes of social service that they had asked Government to carry out in Ipaja. They wanted a hospital. They wanted a piped water supply. If they continued behaving in an irresponsible manner the District Officer would send in an unfavourable report and Government would by-pass their town as far as amenities were concerned.

The little bald-headed old man then said that the Clerk should beg the White Man not to be angry with them at Ipaja. He looked round the assembly, seeking approval from the faces of his fellow-citizens.

Several people now spoke at the same time, some indignant, some fearful of the White Man's anger, some merely shouting incomprehensibly, but all indicating that they did not want their cocoa trees cut.

At this point the proceedings were further interrupted by the entrance of a magnificent figure. He wore English clothes, like Johnson, the District Officer's clerk, but, judging from the superiority of his worsted suit to Johnson's shabby tussore, he was of far greater importance and learning. A walking-stick swung from his right hand and a pipe drooped from his mouth. A grey Bourdillon hat topped his six feet, and he wore black, pointed shoes.

'Mr Benjamin Benjamin!' someone shouted.

'Welcome. Only you can understand the words that the white farmer is saying,' another said as the newcomer proceeded to take his seat on the front bench.

'You have come at just the right moment, Mr Benjamin Benjamin.'

The two white men watched the newcomer take his seat, the younger man with curiosity and a trace of annoyance at this educated black man who insisted on wearing the white man's warm clothes in the hot humid weather. Whatever Stanfield, the District Officer, thought of the new arrival and his clothes, he did not betray it as he watched him to his seat.

'Who is that chap who's just come?' Gregory, the Agricultural Officer, spoke to Stanfield, though his eyes were on Benjamin Benjamin. 'Is he likely to have anything useful to say?'

'Good morning to you, Mr Benjamin Benjamin,' Jim Stanfield said. 'You are not exactly a farmer; you are certainly not a farmer's representative. But now that you are here you may as well let us know what you feel about this terrible disease. Do you agree that these farmers should allow the diseased cocoa trees on their farms to be cut down, in order to save the rest of the trees on their farms? Or should they leave them to spread the disease to the rest? If they choose the first alternative they lose a few trees. If they choose the latter – well, they lose all their farms. Which do *you* advise, Mr Benjamin Benjamin?'

The man rose to speak. First he put down his walking-stick. Then he took out of the breast pocket of his jacket a yellow handkerchief. Next he removed the glasses from his face and proceeded to wipe the lenses with the handkerchief. He replaced the glasses, removed the pipe from his mouth, and picked up the walking-stick again. Finally he began to speak, in English, but through Johnson.

'I bid you greet Mr Stanfield, the District Officer, and his companion Mr Gregory, the Agricultural Officer, in the name of the Oba and Chiefs and people of Ipaja. I bid you tell them that we thank them for the trouble they have taken to come here to talk to us. Tell them that we appreciate their effort. But what we in Ipaja want the Government to do for us is not to cut down our cocoa trees. Government need not do this to demonstrate to us the power of the White Man. We already know that. I bid you tell the District Officer that what we in Ipaja want the Government to do for us now is to take back from the people of Apeno and give to us the Igbodudu land which the Apenos stole from us. We want back the Igbodudu land. That is what we want. Elders and youths of Ipaja, is this not what agitates your minds? Is it not the Igbodudu land you want back from the Apenos?' he demanded with great emotion.

Once again the meeting was roused. They all wanted back the land. They wanted it back immediately.

Igbodudu? Somewhere in Stanfield's memory, a bell rang. There was no point pursuing the subject of cocoa disease. But as he had not come briefed to discuss the disputed land, he declared the meeting closed.

CHAPTER TWO

Back at the bush Rest House on the hill outside the town the District Officer offered his companion a cigarette from a silver case, engraved with his initials. He took one himself. They both smoked in silence for a while.

'Damn it all, man,' Gregory said, throwing his cigarette-end through the window on to the wide concrete veranda. 'It's all wrong. Can't these people see that we're trying to help them?'

'Is it really all that simple?' Stanfield asked reflectively. He wandered out on to the veranda and paced up and down. His companion joined him, offering him a cigarette of his own from a packet which he took from the breast pocket of his shirt.

'If these farmers can't see that all diseased trees must be cut out, the end of the cocoa industry here is absolutely inevitable. And we may as well pack up – book our passages on the next mailboat out. The meeting was going perfectly well until that bloke broke it up. Why in God's name, Jim, can't we put the fellow in custody?'

'Then we really would be landed in trouble,' said the District Officer. He looked down over the quarter-mile of wooded slope which was supposed to protect the Rest House from the malaria-carrying mosquito which infested the town. 'Put Chief Momo of Ipaja in custody! Just what for, Henry?'

'Why, for standing in the way of progress. These bloody Africans need to be protected against themselves, and against their own ignorance. And, damn it,' he continued, 'they need to be protected against our fancy notions of democracy. Just because we in Britain have evolved a system of government by discussion and argument which somehow seems to work we think we must use the same methods in tropical Africa. We think we must get agreement on every measure before we take decisions. But, what's the good of discussion by fellows who don't understand what we are talking about, and persist in misunderstanding our motive?'

'Parliamentary democracy, Henry, is the one great contribution that our country has made to civilization. It's for this that Britain will be remembered long after our empire has passed away.'

'Ah, parliamentary democracy! You fellows in the Administration seem to forget that our parliamentary democracy has taken eight hundred years to evolve. Today the evolution continues. We came to their country only eighty years ago, and all the time we've been teaching them to stop killing one another or selling each other into slavery. And we've been uniting them under one government for the first time —'

'And, incidentally, who did you say that overdressed bastard was that finally put paid to the meeting?'

'Oh,' said Stanfield, 'that was Benjamin Benjamin. A member of the African intelligentsia. A local man, with a good deal of influence over the old Oba and his chiefs. You'll remember the keynote of last year's second Wiltshire Course. In all we do we must carry the intelligentsia with us.'

'Oh that's nonsense. There's nothing intelligent whatever about him. If we have to carry with us every native in coat and trousers who likes to call himself educated, and every bush chief like Momo who scratches the surface of the soil and likes to call himself a farmer – well, I tell you, we'll have lost the race for development in Africa before we ever get started.'

'You mustn't be too impatient with them. I must confess I've some sympathy for Benjamin Benjamin. It's quite a vision, you know, the vision of leading one's people. Don't you see what it means to him?'

'I see. Another Moses leading his people out of the bondage

of imperialism. Tell me something more about the fellow. What's his background?'

'Nothing much, I'm afraid. He had a pretty poor start. Dismissed from elementary school a few months before he was due to take the Standard VI examination. It was over some schoolboy nonsense – a love letter to a girl in the same school.'

'I see, I see.'

'No, I don't think you do. It was all quite harmless, but you know what those old-time Mission teachers are. The headmaster was pretty tough, I understand.

'Then Benjamin Benjamin was job-hunting in Apeno for a long time. Eventually bribed his way into the news department of one of the papers, the *National News*, if I remember rightly. Started as a reporter on social functions – you know the kind of thing. Weddings and funerals. Arrivals from leave or from studies overseas. Departures on transfer —'

'Oh yes, they make a thing of all that in these local papers, don't they?'

'His reports were full of long words and flourishes, the sort of style that newspaper readers lap up. And Benjamin Benjamin was a great favourite of the news editors.' Stanfield stopped to light another cigarette. He smoked a little and hesitated.

'Then, instead of keeping within his safe niche of social gossip, he waded into the deeper waters of nationalism. And, as always happens, he ran foul of the law. It was a long rambling article in which he libelled everyone from the Colonial Secretary and the Governor to the Chief Justice and Commissioner of Police. Dick Battersworth wasn't exactly lenient; he gave him six months.'

'Just as well, too,' commented Gregory.

'No,' said Stanfield. 'He was wrong. With that stiff sentence he was starting the man off on the road to martyrdom.'

'Oh yes?'

'In prison he read a lot of stuff smuggled in to him by newspaper friends and prison warders. He read up about the formation and organization of political parties, the history of underground movements and technique of guerrilla warfare. He himself contributed a thesis on *The Role of the Chief in the Africa of Tomorrow*.'

'Oh yes? And you got all this information while he was in gaol?'

'The C.I.D. boys were quite efficient in this case. Don't forget that the police chief was one of the people Benjamin Benjamin had libelled.

'When he came out of gaol, he stepped back into his job, which they'd kept open for him, and he wrote more and more articles, some under his own name, but a lot under pseudonyms.

'These days, he spends half his time here in Ipaja, and the other half in the Secretariat in Apeno. He is collecting material for writing a history of the Ipaja people. He wants access to the Headquarters intelligence reports, but of course we can't let him have them.'

'Quite a boy!' said Gregory. 'And he's writing a history of his own people d'you say? The last chapter will have to be "The Death of the Cocoa Industry". Look here, Jim, I admit that he's got some personality, and that a colourful character like that may enliven an administrator's drab routine. But really you should recognize the fellow for what he is – a trouble-maker. And the sooner you have him locked up the better. While you have him around loose, and while you pay attention to the nonsensical stalling of these old chiefs and peasants, you'll never get anything done. My God, they are a maddening lot!'

Stanfield shook his head. 'I still feel you're being impatient with these boys, Henry,' he said. 'We mustn't allow our enthusiasm for quick results to kill our capacity for getting any results at all. And that may well happen, unless we're very careful.'

'How's that?'

'You see, we are already dedicated to this policy of planting parliamentary democracy in Africa before we quit, or before we are kicked out, depending on which comes first. And if we are not to be kicked out we must allow the vociferous few who now think for the silent and ignorant many to know just what we're doing and why we're doing it. It's not enough, for instance, that you and I know that diseased trees must be removed today if they're not to bring death to the remainder tomorrow. We must let Momo's brothers, the newspaper editor, the schoolmaster and the Salvation Army leader – all his precious lot of relations who can read and write, however imperfectly – know these facts. We must enlist the support and sympathy of these relatives of Momo to help us carry Momo with us. They're themselves only a little better than Momo in their understanding of the whys and wherefores of everyday things around them. But we must realize that the new race for Africa cannot be won without winning first the mind of the African. Patience, sympathy and understanding – that's what we need.'

'We are already succeeding. I hear an African is taking over the District from you,' the younger man said without attempting to conceal his sarcasm.

'Udo Akpan,' Stanfield said, almost affectionately, 'a magnificent fellow, that.'

'Very magnificent, I gather. Set two clans against each other in his own home district before asking for a transfer away from his mess.'

'You judge Udo much too harshly, Henry.'

'Don't get me wrong. I admire the fellow's brain. An upper second in Classics, I hear. Cambridge cricket blue. Excellent clubman and all that. But what is all that to the half million tribesmen and women who collected the pennies from their purses to award him a scholarship to go and study in England? There wasn't a single person in his headquarters who had heard of cricket before. As soon as the two clans brought to him a small palaver which owing to lack of tact and understanding he magnified into a near-riot, he asked for a transfer to the more peaceful region of the country. I tell you, this experiment just won't work. I'm perfectly certain of it.'

'Udo is a grand man. Got more sense than you think, has Udo. You see, I always thought it was a mistake posting these boys to their own home districts. Certainly not in their first tours, anyway.'

'I should have thought that would be an advantage,' Gregory retorted. 'Let the bloke work where he knows the people and he is known. Why, your precious District Officer here will require an interpreter just as you do: "The Black White Man salutes you, Oba and Chiefs of Ipaja,"' he mimicked in derision.

'I disagree with you. When you meet Udo Akpan you'll revise your opinion of him. His home clans are the descendants of a warrior tribe. Most difficult people. In days gone by Udo might have vanished without a trace. They are getting amenable to Pax Britannica now.'

'Still the fellow ought to have stayed, and worked among his own people. I don't believe in this prophet-not-having-honour-in-his-own-land stuff. Another cigarette?'

CHAPTER THREE

One evening some three weeks after that disastrous meeting the Elders of Ipaja were assembled on the spacious veranda of the royal compound of the Oba of Ipaja. They sat on creaking chairs and benches. He himself sat on a high-backed mahogany chair, on a raised mud dais. In one hand he held a white horse-tail; five heavy silver rings glistened on the fingers of his left hand as it rested on the arm of his chair. He wore a white blouse heavily embroidered in green silk and over the left shoulder was thrown one end of a loose-fitting white velvet wrapper. On his head he wore a small white cap.

At the further end of the veranda three courtiers squatted. There was a keg of palm wine near them, its foaming bubbles indicating that it had not been diluted.

'Elders of Ipaja, I bid you welcome, and I bid you a pleasant evening,' the old chief said, waving the horse-tail. 'It was I who sent for you. I sent for you all to come to my compound. There is cause for my asking you to meet here, in my own compound.' Here he paused to sneeze, which earned him a murmur of congratulation from his chiefs. To sneeze is believed to be an operation for expelling evil through the nose and the mouth. A royal person doing this is therefore congratulated on getting through a successful operation.

'Many moons ago, we used to hold our meeting here, in my compound,' the Apaja continued. 'Here, the first Apaja, the founder of Ipaja, met his chiefs. And here my fathers met their chiefs and discussed state affairs. Now they all sleep there.'

He indicated the furthermost end of the compound where his predecessors on the stool of Ipaja were buried.

'They all sleep there. But they hear everything we say. And they breathe peace. That was why we had peace when we met here, in my compound. But after we built the Court House, we began to meet in the Court House. And since we began to hold meetings in the Court House we have had no peace. We have had no understanding. That is why I ordered my bell crier to summon you all to my compound today. Elders of Ipaja, I bid you all welcome to my compound today. Elders of Ipaja, I bid you all welcome. May the spirit of the founder of Ipaja be with you all.'

After these introductory remarks the Apaja sat back in his chair. One Elder got up and took four long strides in a semicircle to the centre of the group. He lay flat on his stomach in salutation. '*Kabiyesi*, the Owner of Ipaja. Long may the beaded shoes adorn your royal feet. Long may you hold the beaded staff of office, and long may you rule over us. Fellow Elders of Ipaja,' he said, looking round the group from his undignified position, 'will these things come to pass or not?'

They all chorused that these invocations of long life for the head of Ipaja would come to pass. The old man scrambled to his feet, and beat off the dust from his garment with the palm of his right hand. He proceeded to take his seat. His expression of good wishes was apparently sufficient evidence of agreement with the observations of the Head that the veranda of the royal compound provided a more peaceable atmosphere for deliberating serious affairs of state. For the Oba proceeded: 'The Clerk told me that my good friend the District Officer has written to me bad words in a letter. When the Clerk read to me the words of the letter I was sad. For they were bad words; they were angry words. So I sent for you all, Elders of Ipaja, that you may hear these angry words that the District Officer has written to us. I also sent for Benja-Benja, to read the letter to us. He has much greater learning than the Clerk. That is the reason why I sent for Benja-Benja to read the letter to us.'

Benjamin Benjamin proceeded, very noisily, to the foot of the dais. He was as usual dressed in English clothes. He greeted them all with nods right and left. At the foot of the dais he put down his walking stick, and removed the pipe from his mouth and the hat from his head. Then taking three steps backward, he went down flat on his stomach, all six feet of him, coat and trousers and tie notwithstanding. '*Kabiyesi*, my liege lord,' he said. 'Oba Apaja of Ipaja. Descendant of the Founder of the most ancient dynasty on earth. I worship you. I worship the beaded staff in your royal hand. And I worship the beaded shoes on your royal feet . . . I worship the royal ground trodden by your royal feet, the royal words issuing from your royal mouth. Fathers of Ipaja, my humble respects to you all.'

The Apaja waved him up with the horse-tail. 'Get up, get up,' he said. 'People with so much learning like you should not prostrate for too long. Otherwise you suffer from back-ache!'

'His back is now much too stiff for this sort of thing!' one of the Elders remarked.

Getting up, Benjamin Benjamin demanded the letter from the Clerk, produced from his breast pocket a pair of glasses which he adjusted precariously on the bridge of his nose. For a moment he read through the letter in silence, ostentatious nods and frowns indicating his appreciation of an important matter of state. He then proceeded to read aloud the letter in English.

My Good Friend,

The Council Clerk, I trust, will have reported to you the unbecoming behaviour of the representatives of the Ipaja Farmers' Association at the meeting with the Provincial Agricultural Officer on 12 July. This behaviour has brought shame not only to the people who were present at the meeting but to the people of Ipaja as a whole.

2. The Provincial Agricultural Officer is a very busy person. He looks after two provinces of which your division is only one of many divisions. Your Farmers' Union forms only a fraction

of all the farmers in both provinces. In spite of this the Agricultural Officer tore himself away from the very important work at his headquarters and had to motor nearly a hundred miles to come to speak to your farmers. But the Ipaja farmers have shown lack of appreciation of the sacrifice in time that he made. They have also shown an utter ignorance of the cause of the meeting. If they had understood they would doubtless have shown a more reasonable and intelligent attitude.

3. The Government of the country is fully convinced that a very serious disaster threatens your cocoa industry, and therefore your welfare. This Government is spending much money and time to combat the cocoa disease and so save you and your families from disaster. But your representatives have shown by their attitude that your Division does not deserve the consideration that Government intended to give it. Government will of course concentrate its attention on those people who will co-operate with it in its effort to combat the disease, and ignore those people who through ignorance constitute themselves into an obstruction to its work.

4. It may be that the farmers of Ipaja have realized that they have been misled in their attitude and that they have now seen reason. If this is so, Government will be prepared, the Agricultural Officer assures me, to carry on with its proposals. You should ascertain the present attitude and wishes of the farmers of Ipaja and let me know by letter as soon as I return from tour.

Your Good Friend,

Udo Akpan

DISTRICT OFFICER

After he had completed the unnecessary reading in English he translated it sentence by sentence as best as he could into the vernacular. Then followed the debate, opened by the Apaja himself.

'Elders of Ipaja. You have heard the angry words of the White Man. Very angry words. What shall we do?'

'Very angry words. What shall we do?' One old man, toothless and bald-headed, repeated timidly after the Oba.

'We must do whatever the White Man says. He now owns Ipaja. He owns the world,' one Elder observed.

'But we cannot cut down our own cocoa trees, can we?' another observed, bewildered.

'But we must do what the White Man says. If we don't there will be trouble for all of us. I don't want the White Man's trouble.'

There was silence for some time as the men thought. The lantern threw grotesque shadows on the wall. The toothless, bald-headed old man snored softly. Lightning flashes and thunder indicated the approach of a storm.

'Elders of Ipaja, speak out your minds. Shall we cut out our cocoa trees or shall we not? This is a very serious thing. Speak out your minds,' the Oba said.

Benjamin Benjamin stared at the paper in his hand, deep in thought. Then he exclaimed suddenly, 'Just as I thought. You see this date, 24 July 1947,' he said, passing the sheet of paper round the group, indicating with his glasses the date. They were all proud to be taken into his confidence. They strained their eyes and ears. But black or red figures, capital or small letters, all the characters were the same to the Elders of Ipaja. They conveyed to them nothing but mystery, an incomprehensible complication of lines and curves and dots.

'That date is 24 July. That is five days ago. But Stanfield the District Officer left Apeno on 17 July. That was exactly one week before this letter was written. And what is more, that letter was not signed by Stanfield.'

He paused for his statement to take effect. But whatever seemed to Benjamin Benjamin to be obvious did not appear so to the Elders. The fact that Stanfield left Apeno on a certain day and the letter was dated another had no significance for them.

'I shall show you what I mean,' Benjamin Benjamin said patiently. 'This letter was written seven days after Mr Stanfield had left Apeno. Therefore he could not have written it.'

'I see it now! I see it now!' someone said rather proudly. 'The letter was written by the White Man's clerk, after the

White Man had gone to his country to go and rest for three months.' He beamed round the group in proud satisfaction. They all laughed at the simplicity of the thing.

'My Liege Lord, Fathers. This is a serious matter. This letter is written not by the D.O.'s clerk, and yet not by Stanfield, the D.O. that we all know. It is written by Mr Akpan.' He paused for effect. Then he continued. 'I know, City Fathers, that you are anxious to know who this man Akpan is. He is the new District Officer. What is important about this is that he is not a White Man at all.'

He again paused for effect. Then one man said slowly: 'The man is not a White Man. Yet you say he is the D.O. How can that be?' He gaped round his companions. The two things just did not make sense to him.

'If he is not a White Man how can he be the District Officer?'

'Yes, he is not a White Man. Government has decided that when we drive away the White Man we shall have District Officers of our own blood. As you know we already have doctors and many lawyers that are Africans and not White Men.'

One man confirmed that there were already Africans who were doctors. He said he knew the doctor in a town beyond Apeno. He was the son of a man he knew when he was a trader in the town many years before. He said that was many years earlier before his trade had gone down and he had returned to the farm at Ipaja.

Benjamin Benjamin then said that Government had consulted him, as the 'Political Adviser to the Oba and people of Ipaja', before taking the decision to post an African District Officer to their District and he had approved Government's idea after consulting other educated sons of Ipaja abroad. But they gave Government a condition that whoever was posted to the District must be understanding and must identify himself with the aims and aspirations of the people of Ipaja. He wanted his Master and Lord the Oba and the City Fathers to confirm that he had acted correctly.

'Go on, go on!' the Oba said. 'Of course you have acted correctly. You and your companions know what is going on in the world. Do we know or hear anything here?' The Oba looked round the group; no one contradicted him. 'Go on, my son, go on.'

'But, but – but how can a black man be a District Officer?' One of them could not get over his incredulity.

'My Liege Lord, and City Fathers,' Benjamin Benjamin went on. 'That is why I am here in your midst. To show you that the Black Man is the equal of the White Man. What the White Man can do the Black Man can,' he declared, looking in the direction of the incredulous old man. 'We educated sons of Ipaja agreed to have a black District Officer. But we specified one great condition; that he must do what we want him to do for the progress of our fatherland. I regret to say that this letter written by the new District Officer,' and here he waved the letter to his admiring hearers, 'this is not the way an African District Officer should address an august African Oba and his Council of Elders.' He read out to them – in English – the third paragraph. He continued: 'Threat and intimidation. That is what it is. The usual tactics of colonialism and imperialism. Insult and degradation. Yet this is from one of our own colour. We must tell him we shall take no nonsense in this ancient town. As your Political Adviser, I bid you set your royal heart at rest, my Master Liege Lord and you City Fathers. You are safe against the agents of imperialism and colonialism, both white and black. No one is going to touch a single tree, however lowly, on the farm of an Ipaja man. Not when there is still blood in the veins of Benjamin Benjamin, Political Adviser to the Apaja-in-Council.'

The following day a letter was written to the District Officer informing him that the Apaja of Ipaja and his Council of Elders had given the most careful consideration to the points raised by the District Officer in his letter to them. They were unable to agree to the suggestion that they should cut out their cocoa trees for the flimsy reason that they were alleged to be diseased. They thanked the District Officer for his anxiety and interest in the welfare of the people of Ipaja. They would, however, want him to give proof of the professed interest by removing the great wrong which had been committed against the people of Ipaja when the land known as Igbodudu was taken away by the first White Man that came to that area and was given to the Apenos, the life-long enemy of the Ipajas. They hoped that, now that an African was District Officer, he would understand the feeling of the people of Ipaja on this sacred question of their land. 'We want you to know that our stock of patience which is proverbially inexhaustible is nearing exhaustion,' the letter continued. 'So you should use your good influence to see that our land – the land of our fathers, passed on to us legitimately and taken away from us illegitimately – is restored to us legitimately. We are ready to take every constitutional means to get this land restored to us legitimately. And if this fails, we Apajas still know how to punish the Apenos in the way our fathers punished them before the White Man came. The hour of reckoning is approaching between us and the Apenos. You are an African, like us. Half a word is sufficient for the wise.'

CHAPTER FOUR

The cocoa disease was not the only problem that confronted the Administration at Ipaja. James Stanfield had sympathized with young Gregory's disappointment at the way the meeting had flopped. He was much older in the Colonial Administrative Service and knew that nothing in colonial Africa succeeded first time. If it did then Africa would stop being Africa. There would be nothing left for the Stanfields and Gregorys to do in Africa. There would be nothing left for the Haileys and Perhams to write about on Africa. And there would be no Colonial Office left in London to continue annual reports and statistics on the magnitude of the problem of colonial administration and the White Man's burden and the fight that the indomitable British Administration was putting up against cruel nature in Darkest Africa.

In the seventeen days in which Stanfield was handing over to young Udo Akpan, the older man explained to the newcomer the intricacies and some of the rituals of administration.

But his explanations covered much more ground. He told him much that he thought was essential to his success but which he would not find in any books or reports or policy papers. He told him that while he was a white man he thought he was, from many years' experience in East Africa and later in West Africa, qualified to know how Africans thought and behaved. He told Akpan that his appointment to succeed him in Ipaja was the fulfilment of the ambition of his career, that before retiring from the Service he would train and hand over to an able and honest African. He hoped Akpan would regard him as a father and should feel free to ask him any questions whatsoever that he felt would be of assistance to him. He gave him his home address in Sanderstead, Surrey, and asked him to write to tell him from time to time how he was getting on, and he in turn would write to give him advice. 'Udo, my boy,' Stanfield had said as he shook hands with Akpan before he climbed into the passenger's seat in the Hillman Pickup that took him from Ipaja to Apeno on the first leg of the journey to the coast, 'your success is my success. I'm sure the experiment will succeed. It must succeed. Good-bye, Udo, and good luck.'

Udo Akpan accepted Stanfield's offer of friendship with concealed misgiving. He thought he knew his kind from his student days in Britain. They meant well, and spoke well. They invited the African student to their homes to show they regarded him as a fellow human being: his colour did not matter. But Udo always felt that however much they tried there was always an indefinable something that stood in the way of complete understanding between the African and the Englishman, something that always gave the impression even to the most understanding of Englishmen that the outstanding African is an exception, and that beneath his dark skin swarm the germs of savagery and ritual murder and sex.

The new District Officer was going to approach his new duties of African administration in an essentially African way. The first of these problems concerning Ipaja was the Obanla Chieftaincy dispute. He had made a first reading of the case file. He got the essentials but not the details. The pattern quite usual for a chieftaincy dispute: stool has been vacant for sixteen months; twenty-three contestants originally; now reduced to only two; the Oba and kingmakers favour candidate Olowokere. The name means 'the rich man is not small'. (Akpan remembered having come across the name somewhere.) The educated sons of Ipaja at home and abroad support another candidate, a man educated to the sixth standard, and an Assistant Chief Clerk in a government department in Apeno.

'A complicated case, like all chieftaincy cases,' Stanfield had minuted in the file. 'Olowokere is the favourite in Ipaja, the choice of the kingmakers. The Ifa Oracle according to the kingmakers has declared for him. He is not literate, but very popular and wealthy.

'Abosede, the choice of the Ipaja Improvement Union, is not popular with the Oba and Chiefs. They complain that they do not know him well. It is to be noted that literacy, although desirable, is not a condition of chieftancy in accordance with the Chieftaincy Ordinance.'

Another serious headache to which Akpan succeeded in his new duties was the Igbodudu Land Dispute. The recorded life of the problem was thirty-two years older than himself and fifty-eight years older than his appointment as a young cadet in the Administrative Service. In six sheets of typewritten Intelligence Report, half of which had been badly eaten by insects, a predecessor-in-office who signed himself Colonel Higgs had set down details and causes of a disturbance between the villagers of Ipaja and those of Apeno, a day's march away to the east.

Akpan had read the Report once before at the provincial headquarters. He now took the relevant file along with him on his first visit to Ipaja in the hope that reading it in Ipaja itself might give him the added inspiration required to understand the mystery of the missing sheet. This sheet appeared to have been deliberately torn out of the file as there was the stub left. On the unused half of the last sheet was a blurred minute, obviously newer than the main scripts: 'Portion of Report missing. No doubt torn off by someone deliberately to frustrate my effort to solve the mystery of the Igbodudu Land Dispute. Packing up and going back to my Sally, before I go crazy. Can't stand it any more.' This unorthodox minute was followed by a sketch of a girl holding the lead of a spaniel against the background of an English cottage in winter. She wore a blouse and skirt, and had a pretty face; no administrator in His Majesty's Colonial Service could really be blamed for returning to such a face. But Udo Akpan was not just any administrator. He swore he must get to the bottom of the mystery of the Land Dispute.

While his trusted steward battled to get the Tilley gas lamp lighted, Akpan mapped out his line of attack. He asked his police orderly to find out from the Rest House caretaker which of the churches in the town was called St John's.

'St John's?' The caretaker said he knew St John's and if the black White Man wanted him to he could take him to the church.

'In which direction do we go?'

'In which direction? Why, there, of course,' the old man said, describing with a sweep of his hand about half the horizon.

'Ask him, orderly, does he know the Catholic Church too?'

'The Catholic Church? Of course I do. And if Master wants I can take him there too.'

Akpan looked at him intently for a moment before he asked:

'And where is the Catholic Church? Ask him.'

'Where is the Catholic Church? Why, there, of course!' the caretaker said, with another sweep of his hand covering about the same area as before, perhaps a little less definite.

'You are a fool,' the orderly told the caretaker in the vernacular. 'And I tell you you've lost your job, bush man. And I advise you not to play with this District Officer just because he is a black District Officer. You must give him intelligent answers.'

Akpan saw he could not trust the caretaker for guidance in finding the church he wanted. He decided to trust to his own devices for finding it when he got into the middle of the town.

After his supper of stewed chicken and boiled rice, washed down with a glass of Bordeaux wine smuggled across the border from French West Africa, he set out with the orderly in his 1945 Ford Prefect down the dusty laterite road that wound round the wooded slopes that lay between the Rest House and the town. The car swerved to avoid sheep and goats caught in the powerful beams of the headlights. They huddled together in little groups, wholly unaware of the peril lurking behind the headlights. Akpan reflected on the inability of animals to learn from bitter experience, for he remembered that on more than one occasion he had seen lorry drivers, less mindful than an administrative officer, kill or maim these uncared-for domestic animals.

He noticed groups of children playing games or telling folk-tales on verandas, dimly lit by clay lamps that burnt palm oil. He wondered whether it would really happen that Ipaja, in his District, would sometime enjoy the benefits of electricity, a report on which (according to the Handing-Over Notes) had gone up to the Provincial Headquarters as part of the projected Five-Year Development Programme. It occurred to him momentarily that he had not made an appointment with the vicar of the church. He might be away, or he might be keeping some other appointment. An Englishman would not make an official call in England without a previous appointment. But then this was Africa, his own Africa, not England. In this happy land the doors of the house of a citizen are open to a fellow citizen at any time of the day. The hospitality of the house of a true African is open to anyone, native or stranger, any time of the day. He knew at once that the District Officer was welcome in all homes in Ipaja – except in the homes of criminals or tax-evaders.

He sought direction twice, once from a sales clerk who took the opportunity to demonstrate to those around his knowledge of English by using long words and involved sentences. On the second occasion, his guide, a schoolboy, jumped at the offer of a free ride to St John's Church and parsonage.

The car under the pilotage of the schoolboy stopped outside the parsonage.

'This is the pastor's house, sir,' the boy said.

Akpan came out and held the door open for both the boy and the orderly. Already a crowd of curious children had formed round them. One or two shouted the name of the schoolboy guide. To these the favoured boy smiled importantly as he led the way to the parsonage steps. But the District Officer did not follow his guide up the steps of the parsonage immediately. He lingered behind studying the new church building under construction. He saw the great stone arches and the massive concrete columns on which they were carried. He saw the timber framework and the bamboo scaffolding. He saw the roof trusses being assembled on the church grounds and heard the noise that some dozen or so carpenters and their mates made nailing these together. He was not an expert in building or architecture but even from a distance he noticed a number of things that did not appear pleasing to the eye in the new building. He reflected on the great act of faith that formed the very foundations of these church building projects, the faith which prompted church congregations to embark upon projects that would cost several thousand pounds before they had as much as a hundred pounds in the kitty. The faith that made them trust to the annual harvest thanksgiving offerings and the attendant bazaar sales, to the New Year offerings from the faithful and the occasional pound or two from the devoted son of the soil who had made good in a distant trading station.

The vicar was not in, but the sexton was found. He said that the vicar had not gone far and he would go and call him from the vestry where he was having discussions with two church elders.

While he was waiting for his host to come from the church vestry Udo Akpan made himself as comfortable as he could in the sitting-study room of the Mission House. He looked at the pictures in the Churchman's Calender which was nailed to the wall. He saw, staring at him as if in rebuke, the face of His Grace the Archbishop of the province. Ringed round him were the clerics and divines of the various churches of the diocese. Udo Akpan was not a churchman even though he had attended a church school in his own part of the country. He had been completely indifferent to the doings of these dignitaries of the church. In the four years when he worked as a junior clerk in a Government office before he was awarded a Government scholarship to study in the United Kingdom he had not been affected by that arm of the nationalist movement that was condemning missionary activities in the country. In the United Kingdom he had attended student union meetings where budding nationalists read long theses to prove that the church missions were in fact an advance army of the British imperialist and that their real mission was to prepare the mind and keep the eye of the converted African on the blessings of the Kingdom in heaven while the British imperialist carried away the good things of the kingdom here on earth. In spite of the considerable effects of this movement on some of his fellow students, Udo Akpan had remained moderate in his political views.

'Good evening, brother,' Josiah Olaiya said, as he came in, 'and the Lord be with you.'

'Good evening, Pastor,' Akpan said, rising and taking three steps towards his host. He offered his hand.

'I apologize, Sir, for not letting you know in advance that I was coming to see you. My name is Udo Akpan; I am the new District Officer.'

The clergyman pressed the hand of his visitor with brotherly warmth.

'You are welcome, sir, to the lowly abode of a parish priest. This, brother, is a great honour to Mrs Olaiya and myself. Please sit down. This chair,' he said pushing the most presentable of the three cane chairs towards his visitor. . . . 'That other one has been damaged. Sit down, and be comfortable, sir.'

Akpan sat down. And he conveyed the impression of being comfortable. He took out his cigarette case.

'I see you smoke a pipe, sir. But may I offer you a cigarette? You will like it, I am sure.'

'I do not smoke cigarettes, brother. I am happy with my pipe. When I smoke it, I think clearly.'

'May I smoke my cigarette, then? When I talk to important people, smoking a cigarette makes my thoughts flow properly.'

'Please smoke your cigarettes, brother, while I smoke my own pipe. It is a pity Mrs Olaiya is out now at a meeting of the Mothers' Union. She would have loved to meet such an august visitor as you, sir. Even though she is not in, I hope you will taste of her orange juice.'

After a drink of home-made orange juice which Akpan pretended to enjoy, he said, 'I am sure you will understand why I have come to see you on the occasion of my first visit to Ipaja. My appointment as District Officer is an experiment. And I want to do everything to make the experiment succeed, in the interest of the black man. I know that without the cooperation and guidance of the few Africans like you who combine education with age, the experiment cannot succeed. May I therefore from time to time call upon you for advice?'

The older man merely nodded. He was apparently overcome by the humility and the desire of the younger man for cooperation. Akpan went on:

'I know that you have been in Ipaja for many years. I know that you know the people not only inside the church but outside it as well. You know their history and their customs. A particular problem now confronting the Administration is the land dispute between the people of Ipaja and those of Apeno. I am sure there are among your church elders some who are old enough and would be willing to give a true account of the history of the disputed land. Their account given to you will be reliable. If I ask them for the same information they will be suspicious of my motive and will not give me reliable information. I am sure you will be willing to help the Administration in this respect. Needless to say, sir, any information you give in this respect will be treated with the utmost confidence.'

Josiah Olaiya did not speak for some time after his visitor

had finished speaking. He smoked pensively. Then he rose to his feet slowly and began to pace up and down his study.

'I scarcely believe it, sir. I am happy that I have lived to see this day, when a man of my own colour is the District Officer. Praise to the Lord God of Hosts who has made me live to see this day, when I, a lowly parish priest, have been considered worthy to be paid a visit by the first African District Officer in the land – I, Josiah Olaiya, without a university degree, neither a doctor nor a lawyer.

'As for the history of the Igbodudu land, I shall get one of our church elders to tell it to me. And I shall write it out for you. There is no bit of the history of this land that Chief Momo does not know. He is a man you must know, brother.'

After a few more minutes of general discussion, Udo Akpan bade his host good night.

On his way back to the Rest House Akpan had to stop his car on the main street to make room for a large car, whose approach was heralded by much hooting and shouting. Akpan noticed that there was a definite rhythm to the hooting – two long blasts followed by three short ones. This, together with shouts of 'Olowo!' which preceded the car brought children from their games thronging the verandas, joining in the shout: 'Olowo!'

'What is it all about?' Akpan asked his orderly, as the car approached slowly.

'It is Olowo, the rich man.'

'The rich man,' Akpan muttered as he watched an Oldsmobile saloon, the newest model, approach and pass him where he was parked, the lone occupant on the back seat waving to him in a dignified, patronizing manner.

Akpan did not discourage the orderly who had welcomed the opportunity of the D.O.'s question to tell him more about Olowokere. He was the wealthiest man in the country. He was a millionaire. He had recently joined the millionaire's club on his last visit to Apeno. He had paid a million pounds for the car, which was the longest car in the world. Only millionaires were allowed to buy the car, and ride in it. . . . Olowo was very rich indeed. He would have gone to England, to the White Man's country, but for the Obanla chieftaincy dispute. Now that the Governor had signed his appointment papers as Chief Obanla, he would soon go to England.

CHAPTER FIVE

Udo Akpan did not have a very good night, thanks to the full moon shining straight into the Rest House through uncurtained windows, to the discordant chorus of a tribe of frogs in the near-by stream, and to the night watchman who was demonstrating to the new District Officer his efficiency by doing a round of the Rest House at frequent intervals in the night.

Akpan was just on the verge of sleep, in spite of the crowing of what sounded like the entire cock population of Ipaja, when he was once more brought back to earth by the beams of a pair of searchlights shining through the windows and bathing the room with light. The noise of the approaching car aroused him thoroughly. It drew up in the drive.

The District Officer could refuse to see anyone at that inconvenient hour of the morning, but this time he did not choose to. For one thing, the visitor, whoever he was, must have seen him scrambling out of bed in the scanty privacy of the Rest House. However, he, took his time over dressing before strolling into the sitting-room.

Two men who were sitting there rose at his approach. One of them introduced himself and his companion:

'Good morning, D.O. I am Benjamin Benjamin. And this, D.O., is Mr Olowokere, Managing Director of Olowokere Transport.'

'Good morning to you, Mr Benjamin Benjamin,' Udo Akpan said, shaking Benjamin's hand. 'And good morning to you, sir.' He shook the hand of the other visitor. 'You have come rather early. Very important matter, no doubt.'

'It is the custom of our fathers, D.O., to transact very important business of state at dawn. In our country we settle important quarrels at dawn. We call important family meetings at dawn.'

'I see,' Akpan said, slightly nettled at the man's manner.

'And meeting the first African D.O., welcoming him to the ancient town of Ipaja – why, it is such an important event that it must be done at cockcrow, before the mouth speaks other words. And I have come on behalf of the Oba and elders and people of Ipaja, and in the company of the wealthiest and most enlightened citizen of Ipaja, to extend to you, D.O., the right hand of fellowship and of cooperation.' Here Benjamin Benjamin again shook hands with Akpan. He continued: 'We as Africans have one common cause, the expulsion of the White Man from this land. And we must pull together in the joint venture, D.O. You must have confidence in me, and I have confidence in you. Confidence begets – confidence, ha, ha!'

'Thank you,' Akpan said, betraying his disappointment at the emptiness of the purpose of the visit. 'And what can I do for you?' he asked switching attention from the self-important Benjamin Benjamin.

'Mr Olowokere does not speak English, but he is a most enlightened citizen nevertheless, with very progressive ideas. You no doubt have heard that he is the choice of the entire people of Ipaja for the Obanla chieftaincy. Most suitable for the chieftaincy. Everyone wants him. It is amazing how the entire people just sing his praises —

'Of course he has not come this morning to plead his case for the chieftaincy. He has come with me just to welcome and give respect to the first African D.O. in the land. You no doubt will wish to reciprocate the respect the chief-designate has shown you. . . . You will find set out here' – and here he produced from the inside of his waist pocket an envelope which he offered to Akpan – 'some useful information about the Obanla Chieftaincy and related matters.'

'Mr Benjamin Benjamin, I appreciate your motive in trying to assist and I must thank you. But really, documents like this should be submitted in the office.'

'If you do not take it, Mr Olowokere will consider it a personal insult to him. And I suggest that you and I will get on well together if we do not stand on form. Above all your Chief Clerk must not know what goes on between you and me. I think we must leave you now to go and get ready for the office. Good morning, D.O. We see in the office.'

Again and again Udo Akpan weighed the matter over in his mind as he prepared to leave for the office. Again and again he came to the conclusion that he had made a bad start with Benjamin Benjamin, and he blamed himself for it. He was D.O. and he must build round himself some amount of prestige. It was a mistake that he had made himself available to those who called without any appointment. And at such an inconvenient hour too. And, to add insult to injury, the fellow had the audacity to deliver to him personally in the Rest House an official document that should go through the normal processes of bureaucracy in the office. He sighed in self-condemnation for his indiscretion.

As Udo Akpan was sulking over the failure of his encounter, Benjamin Benjamin and Olowokere were celebrating the success of their mission to the D.O. They were drinking whisky in the first-floor sitting-room of the transport magnate.

'Benja-Benja, I confess I was afraid when we were driving up the hill. I said to myself: "Supposing he arrests us, what shall we do?" But Benja-Benja, you are very bold.'

'You see, we must not be afraid of these people. Even when the white D.O. was here you know how I treated him. He is a servant of the people. And he must be told that always.'

'Benja-Benja!' Olowo said in admiration of the man who would put the D.O. in his place.

'And once you let them know you will take no nonsense and that they must accept you as their equal you will find that all these senior civil servants from the Resident down to the new

D.O. will respect you.' He gulped a mouthful of whisky to emphasize his point.

'And I was afraid he would call the police after you gave him the money. There is nothing that money will not do.'

'I told him that the money was for drinks. I told him not to open the envelope till we were gone. He said I should thank you for the kola.'

'Benja-Benja! You know how to do it. All the fifty pounds was in the envelope?'

'All the fifty pounds.'

'And you think he will now support my candidature? He will write good things about me to the Resident? You think that he will not say that I have no school education? Do you think the fifty pounds is enough, Benja-Benja, or should I give you some more for the D.O.?' And without waiting for an answer he rose and went to the drawer of a side table from which he took out a bundle of red currency notes. He counted twenty notes and gave the rest to Benjamin Benjamin. 'Here is another thirty pounds. Twenty-five for the D.O. And five for you, Benja-Benja. For all your trouble. And when the whole thing comes through you will have your reward in full. . . . Benja-Benja, why does anyone have money if he cannot spend it to buy the desires of his heart? I have houses. I have women, and children. I have seven lorries and two cars. . . . The one thing that remains for me to achieve in this world is to become a chief. And whatever it costs me, Benja-Benja, I must become the Obanla, second in rank to the Oba himself.'

'And you shall, my chief,' Benjamin Benjamin assured him. 'While I remain the Political Adviser to the Oba and people you will be the Obanla.'

Benjamin Benjamin staggered out of the house of Olowo, full of whisky and extremely pleased with himself, satisfied in the knowledge that Olowo had no idea that the envelope contained only a petition about the chieftaincy and no money at all.

CHAPTER SIX

At the Court House the Oba of Ipaja and his chiefs were meeting the new District Officer at the instance of the latter. The Oba was seated in his high state chair on the platform, and on his right and in another state chair sat the District Officer. In six chairs ranged on both sides of the Oba and the District Officer sat the chiefs, in the order of their seniority. At the foot of the platform squatted the Court Messengers, carrying the fans and the umbrellas of the chiefs.

Benjamin Benjamin, self-styled Political Adviser to the Oba and chiefs of Ipaja sat in a conspicuous place in the front but below the platform. The benches in the main body of the building were occupied by people who had come more to see the black District Officer than to listen to the proceedings of his meeting with the Oba and the chiefs.

The most junior of the chiefs opened the proceedings by making the usual invocations of long life for the Oba. He then beckoned to one of the boys who squatted at the foot of the platform. The boy came up the platform, carrying a covered calabash, which he handed over to the chief. He opened it and from it brought out two big kola nuts. These he handed, kneeling, to the Oba. The Oba regarded them for a moment. Then he said: 'I invoke the spirit of Igbodudu and the founder of Ipaja to be with us. I call my father and his predecessors on the throne of Ipaja to share in our deliberations. If there be anyone here with an evil mind, let him choke after partaking of these kola nuts. And let his spirit roam about the earth condemned.' He then split the nuts into sections. He selected one for himself, invited Udo Akpan to select one and then gave the rest to the Chief for distribution among his colleagues. Akpan followed the lead of the Oba and the rest of them and chewed his bit with simulated enthusiasm.

After the ritual of the kola nuts was over the Oba said: 'Elders of Ipaja, I want you to listen to the words of the black White Man. I want you to listen to him carefully. He sent a message to me that he wanted to speak to me and to all of you. That is the reason why we have come to meet here this morning. I therefore want you to listen to his words.'

The District Officer rose to speak:

'I salute you, my good friend, the Oba of Ipaja. I salute you, Chiefs of Ipaja. And I salute you, gentlemen,' he said in the direction of Benjamin Benjamin. The District Officer could not see the qualification of the man for being there. But as there were others in the body of the court-house that were not chiefs he was not going to stir up trouble by asking Benjamin Benjamin to leave. Besides, the man was recognized by the Oba, whose confidence he enjoyed. He continued after the Council Clerk had indicated that he had finished interpreting his greetings in the vernacular.

'I am glad of this opportunity to meet you here in your own town of Ipaja. I have had the opportunity of seeing a number of you chiefs at the headquarters office at Apeno. But as this is the first time that I am addressing you as a body in your own town I say "Greetings to you". I am sure we will all cooperate in the task of administering this district with wisdom and justice, for the welfare and happiness of the people of Ipaja.'

After dwelling on a number of harmless subjects, the District Officer said: 'I have to remind you, Obas and Chiefs, that you are under oath to administer native law and custom with justice. I went through the records of a number of cases that were the subject of appeal to me from your Native Court. It was quite obvious that in a number of these cases justice has not been done. I am quite certain that you, chiefs, have failed to take into consideration all the evidence before you in arriving at your decisions. I have found it difficult to understand in one or two cases the reasons why you reversed judgements which from the records of evidence before the Court appear quite just, when there was no record of fresh evidence to necessitate a change of decision. These are changing times, and you, Oba and Chiefs, must learn to change with the times. The things Chiefs did in the past, which went unchallenged by the people of Ipaja of those times, are no longer good enough and will be unacceptable to the new generation of people of Ipaja. In particular, I impress upon you the necessity to overhaul completely your ideas of the administration of justice. Judgement must be given in favour of the party that has right on his side. It does not matter which side has might on his side . . .'

Here he paused to mop his forehead before continuing:

'I must now turn to the question of tax assessment and tax collection. I wish it were not necessary for me to say the things I now have to say, but I must express my utter dissatisfaction with the way you have gone about everything connected with taxation this year. Everything, including the assessments, the appeals. And above all, tax collection. I am quite satisfied that many of the appeals that have been allowed by you are groundless. It is my duty to remind you, chiefs, of your duty to distinguish between a genuine case of hardship and a case of pretended hardship. All connected with tax assessment and tax appeals must be honest in their approach to their duties and arrive at their decisions without fear or favour. I regret to say that, from my examination of the records of the tax appeals kept by the Clerk, I have had to set aside nearly all the revised assessments of you chiefs. I have decided to let the original assessments stand in many cases.' Here he paused for some time for the Council Clerk to catch up with him. Then he continued: 'If anything, many people were under-assessed in the first instance.

'People who are rich must be ready to pay substantial taxes

for the development of their towns and for the provision of social amenities for the community in which they live. And everyone, rich or poor or of adequate means, must pay in proportion to their means. It is a sign of lack of civic sense for anyone to evade tax. People who want progress and amenities must pay for them. You cannot ask for progress and independence with one voice and at the same time refuse to accept the responsibilities that come with progress and independence. The old White Man's rule is now gradually giving way to self-rule. We now see and do many things that are symbolic of the changing order of things. It must not be said that the African is not capable of ruling himself because he is incompetent or because his society is inherently corrupt.

'I salute you, Oba and Chiefs, and commend these matters to you for serious consideration.' He sat down, exhausted, wiping the beads of perspiration from his forehead.

It was in silence that the Oba and his chiefs listened to the speech of the District Officer. The silence continued for a short while after he had sat down. Then the old Oba looked round his chiefs: 'Elders of Ipaja, these are very serious words that the black White Man has spoken to us. What shall we do about them? What reply shall we give him, Elders of Ipaja?' he said wearily. 'Speak out your minds.'

One of the chiefs said: 'My Liege Lord, Master of Ipaja. This man that addressed us a short while ago, this man that said all those things – this man is not an African at all. He is truly a White Man. We must be careful not to be deceived by the colour of his skin. Do you not notice his face?' he asked seriously, looking at the District Officer. 'This is not an African, I tell you.'

'He is not one of our own tribe,' another observed regretfully. 'We do not understand his language. He does not understand ours. How then can he see things like us?'

Udo Akpan wondered why the Clerk was not interpreting. One of them addressed the Clerk: 'Please help me beg the black White Man not to change the decisions of the Assessment

Committee. Tell him that I am an old man and therefore the seventeen shillings and sixpence you first wrote against my name should be written off. I am an old man, you see. Tell the black White Man that I can no longer work as I used to on the farm.'

'Elders of Ipaja,' the Oba said again. 'What shall we do? Shall we pay what we were asked to pay originally? Or shall we beg the black White Man to have mercy on us? Elders, we are all here now, and the black White Man is here too. And the spirit of the Igbodudu is among us. Let us say whatever is in our minds now.'

'I have no money to pay. We must beg the black White Man.'

'I am going to speak out my mind,' Chief Momo rose to speak. 'And I am going to speak like a man, and a chief of Ipaja. My Lord and Master, you and your chiefs amaze me. Why do we all talk like women and children? Why are we afraid of this young man, the black District Officer? When we had White District Officers in the past, did we not have our tax assessments reduced?' He looked round at their faces and he read both confirmation and condemnation. He went on: 'Who in Ipaja does not know that the first assessment is always too high? When the Clerk first writes down three pounds for you, do you not go to beg the Chiefs and do you not go to see the Clerk at home? When you do this, do they not have mercy on you and do they not ask you to pay fifteen shillings instead of the original three pounds? And after paying the kola for the Oba and Chiefs and the Clerk, you still pay less than the original three pounds which the Clerk first writes against your name. And everyone is happy – you, the Oba and Chiefs – and is the Clerk not happy?' and he looked at that worthy who in his embarrassment was scribbling nonsense on the foolscap sheet before him.

'Now because we have a black District Officer, we must pay oppressive taxes —

'But I warn you that this man who addressed us a short

while ago is only black in skin. We must not be deceived. We must not make the mistake of thinking that he is one of us.

'Of course, he is not one of *us*,' Chief Momo continued, contemptuously gesticulating threateningly towards the District Officer. 'If his father were one of us, and present here today, he would have shown more concern about our difficulties.'

'Elders of Ipaja,' the Oba said rather anxiously, 'please speak out your minds. But whatever you do, do not abuse the father of the black White Man. It is not good to bring his father into this —'

Udo Akpan could no longer resist the curiosity to want to know what they were all saying. He had up till then kept the serenity expected of his high office. But the way Chief Momo spoke and pointed at him made him ask the Clerk to let him know what the chief was saying.

The Council Clerk rose to the occasion. He said the chief was saying that the subject was so important that they would find it impossible to reach a wise decision immediately, particularly if the D.O. remained with them.

'In that case I shall leave you, Oba and chiefs, to continue. And you will write to me, Mr Johnson, the result of their deliberations.' He shook hands with the Oba, who opened his mouth as he watched the D.O. gather his papers and proudly walk out of the assembly.

Chief Momo was the first to speak after the District Officer had left. 'The way he left so abruptly indicates that he has no respect for anyone,' he observed.

'He greeted me. He shook hands with me,' the Oba said. 'But Benja-Benja, what shall we do? Why do you not tell us what we should do, Benja-Benja?'

It was unusual for Benjamin Benjamin to wait till he was invited before he joined in a discussion of this nature. Today it suited him to let the Oba and Chiefs find themselves helpless and discover that they had need to call on him for a solution to their problem. He prostrated before the Oba and said the usual salutations. Rising, he said: 'There is great wisdom behind the ancient prayer – may the community never be wanting in Elders. I pray that our community here in Ipaja may never be wanting in Elders of the wisdom and calibre of Chief Momo. To him I say well done . . .

'Now more than ever I do not regret my decision to come and stay with you Elders in the intricate business of piloting the ship of state in these modern times. It is my duty to point out to you, my master, your rights against any administrative officer, white or black, who attempts to undermine your authority over your subjects. Under Native Law and Custom you and your Chiefs have complete authority over your subjects. Udo Akpan is merely interfering with Native Law and Custom. This is contrary to the terms of the Treaty of Friendship between the ancient Kingdom of Ipaja and the Kingdom of Britain. These are things that he does not know and they must be brought to his notice. I am writing a letter to the Resident today to give Udo Akpan more lectures on these important matters. . . . On the question of taxes, it is you who live here always and know your people and what they can pay, who should decide what taxes they should pay, not the inexperienced District Officer. Are you satisfied that the original tax assessments were fair and reasonable?'

'They were not fair and reasonable. I cannot find the money with which to pay mine.'

'Does anyone here want to pay the original assessments?'

'No. Please beg the District Officer to agree that I should not pay the seventeen shillings and sixpence written against my name.'

'We are not going to beg him. We are going to tell him that we are simply going to pay the revised assessments. And that is all. And if he tries to make trouble, we shall test the case in a court of law.'

'Benja-Benja,' one of the chiefs said in admiration.

'Elders of Ipaja, you have heard Benja-Benja,' the Oba said. 'What shall we do? Shall we pay the original assessment?'

'No! No!'

'Do you want the Clerk to write it in his book then that you do not agree with the black White Man? We must be careful in whatever we do. Elders, what shall we do?'

Benjamin Benjamin answered for them. 'Clerk, you are to record in your book that the Oba and Chiefs of Ipaja, at a council meeting this day, and in the presence of representatives of the citizens of Ipaja, have decided to abide by the decisions of the Tax Assessment Appeal Committee and that they reject in its entirety the original assessment. The District Officer is requested to note this and to respect the wishes of the people of Ipaja.'

That night, stretched on the mat on the floor at the side of a smouldering log, the old Oba dreamt an unhappy dream. He dreamt that he was being chased by white men, very many of them. He looked round for his chiefs and his subjects. They were nowhere to be seen. All around him, before him and behind him as far as he could see, they were all white faces, full of hatred for him, speaking angrily in their strange language. Where were his own people – his chiefs and his subjects? He called for them. They were nowhere to be seen. He called for Benjamin Benjamin. He was nowhere to be seen. He called for Johnson, the Council Clerk. He called for his wives, for his children. He called for everybody. They were all gone. Then he fled himself. But he could not go far in any direction because the circle of white faces closed in on him. Then he thought he recognized one of them. Udo Akpan. He was puzzled. For this face was surely that of Akpan. The tribal marks on it were there to identify it beyond all reasonable doubt. But that face was white, like all the other faces. And like the others around he too was making it impossible for him to escape. He cried to him for mercy, but Udo Akpan laughed loud at his misery. And, at his bidding, four of the men around him rushed at the old man and bound his wrists.

After he had recovered from his nightmare, the old man thought the thing over in his ancient mind, and was much troubled. He came to the conclusion that Udo Akpan was indeed a white man in a black man's skin and was capable of exiling him from the throne of his fathers.

CHAPTER SEVEN

One night, not long after the departure of the new District Officer from Ipaja, the town-crier of Ipaja walked through the unlit streets. The kon-kon sound of the hollow metal of his bell rent the night air. The citizens of Ipaja stopped whatever they were doing and stood quietly to listen to the message from the Oba.

'Greetings to you all, sons and daughters of Ipaja,' the crier intoned from the dark of the night. 'To them that have been to the farm, welcome. To them that have been to fetch water from the streams, welcome. To them that have been to sell and to buy at the markets, welcome. My Liege Lord, the Owner of Ipaja has a message for you all. He bids you all, elders and youths of Ipaja, men and women, assemble at the market place tomorrow morning at sunrise. There must be no feet missing at the meeting place. There must be no faces missing at the meeting place. Whoever absents himself incurs the displeasure of the gods. And he shall pay the penalty in goats. Sons and daughters of Ipaja, sons and daughters of Ipaja, elders and youths of Ipaja. The words of the message are finished. Greetings.'

KON – KON – KON! – KON – KON – Kon! – kon – kon – kon!
KON – KON – KON! – KON – KON – Kon! – kon – kon – kon!

Whenever the Oba Apaja of Ipaja wanted to summon his subjects to a palaver or to attend a festival, he bade the town-crier beat his bell and cry out the message from street to street at night, and so it was done on this occasion. But Benjamin Benjamin considered that the importance of the occasion called for something more than ordinary methods. He decided to introduce what he described as an element of civilization to supplement tradition. Some days before he had written out a long and elaborate circular letter under his own signature and the thumb impression of the Apaja of Ipaja. This went out to all sons and daughters of Ipaja at home and abroad. It bade them attend at the market place a mass meeting at which would be discussed a most important matter of state that would affect the future prosperity and happiness of the people of Ipaja in particular and of the country as a whole. All true patriots, men and women, the aged and the young, the rich and the poor, whatever their estate, must make their way to the market place for this most important meeting. Distance must be no barrier – the love of country transcends the physical handicap of distance. It went on like this at some length.

There was a good turnout of Ipaja men and women at the meeting; mostly it was the usual crowd that worshipped in the three churches of different denominations in the town, but there were a few representatives of the category described as Ipaja sons abroad. There were traders in near-by towns and villages. One man had wangled a sick leave and had come all the way from across the River Niger from a town where he was a staff clerk in the employment of the Railway Department.

The Apaja ostensibly presided over the meeting, but Benjamin Benjamin in truth directed the affairs. He opened the proceedings in grand style.

'*Kabiyesi*, Your Most Ancient Highness, the Owner of Ipaja, the Terror of the Apenos, I worship you. Representative of the gods here on earth, the Beloved descendant of the Founder of the world, I worship you. Most handsome of men on earth, Most valiant of swordsmen, Victor of the Battle of Kiriji, the name from which the Oba of Apeno shrinks in terror – your sons and daughters here assembled before you worship you.' As practical evidence of that worship Benjamin Benjamin, today in a rich damask *agbada* and wearing a long gold chain round his neck, prostrated himself and grovelled on the floor.

'May the beaded crown adorn your sacred head for ever,' he continued, still grovelling on the ground.

'So will it be!' chorused the crowd.

'May the beaded shoes adorn your royal feet for ever.'

'So will it be.'

'May you hold for ever in your royal hand the beaded staff of office.'

'So will it be! So will it be! Amen! Amen!'

On his feet once more, Benjamin Benjamin addressed the crowd. 'Sons and daughters of Ipaja, patriots, comrades in the fight for the restoration of the former greatness of Ipaja, my master your father, Lord, Most Ancient Highness, King of Ipaja, bids me say welcome to you all.'

'*Kabiyesi*,' the crowd chorused.

'To those of you in whom the fire of patriotism burns with such great heat that you have left your daily bread to answer the call of patriotism, the King says, "welcome, and well done".'

'*Kabiyesi*, long may he reign!'

'And to those of you, fathers and mothers, who for the sake of fatherland have left your farms, your weaving, and your markets to come to answer the call of our King, he bids me say to you, "Thank you".'

'Kabiyesi! God of Ipaja.'

'And to our chiefs, our fathers who stay at home to carry on the delicate affairs of state under the divine guidance of the King, their Lord and Master – we all say, thank you!'

'May their fathers in heaven support them!'

'Welcome to you all. Welcome one, welcome two, welcome all!'

After this Benjamin Benjamin held a whispered conversation with the Oba, who addressed the gathering next.

'My children —' he said, waving the horse-tail.

'*Kabiyesi* —' the crowd cried in jubilation. He waved the

horse-tail vigorously while Benjamin Benjamin clapped his hands and shouted and implored people to pray be silent for the Oba to continue.

'My children, both men and women, old and young, I greet you all. I say to you all, welcome.'

'*Kabiyesi!*'

'Both natives, and strangers, I bid you all welcome . . . I do not want you young educated men to despise us, your chiefs and old men. You all must behave with respect to us elders . . . like Benja-Benja. He respects us, and he is not arrogant to us in spite of the amount of knowledge he carries in his head. . . . I want you to tell the White Man to stop worrying me in my town. I am king here. Also you should write a letter to him to tell him to give me more money.' The old man looked round at his chiefs, who nodded approvingly. 'My chiefs all want to be paid salaries. We are all hungry. He has stopped all the things that used to bring us food. Tell the White Man to give us money that we may spend to buy food for our stomachs, and live and not die, that we may buy nice clothes to wear and not shame you. My children, my words are finished.'

Here Benjamin Benjamin held a hurried and anxious conversation with the old chief, his gestures emphasizing the importance of what he was telling the Oba. Both he and the Oba eventually succeeded in restoring silence after the prolonged shouts of '*Kabiyesi*' that followed the Oba's speech. Then the Oba made good his omission. 'There is one important matter that I want to tell you. It is the matter of Igbodudu. That land is mine. It was the battle-ground of Igbodudu from where my father drove out the Apenos. The Apenos – they ran like rats, when our soldiers were chasing them out of the land. The Apenos have now taken the land from me. I want you to write to the White Man to take the land back from the Apenos. Tell the White Man to give it back to me. It is my land. My words are finished!'

Another chief took the floor. After paying the usual homage to the Apaja, and bidding welcome all the sons and daughters of Ipaja, he gave the meeting the information that the Apenos their neighbours were a breed of thieves and vagabonds, that the first Apeno was a thief and that it was because of this that he was driven away from the palace of the founder of the major dynasty and banished to Apeno. They therefore should do the right and only thing by taking back from the Apenos the Igbodudu land which had been stolen from them the Apajas.

Benjamin Benjamin again took the floor. He told his admirers that their decision to drive away the Apenos from the Igbodudu required a weapon with which all modern battles were fought and won – money. They required a good amount of money to take the case to the highest Court in the land. They had to engage the services of the most brilliant lawyers. 'This is a battle in which all Ipajas will have a chance of taking part – men and women, old and young, rich and poor. We must all play our parts so that we may all be proud of having contributed something towards the winning back of the land.'

Benjamin Benjamin then announced that the Oba, as a true leader of his people, had promised to open the Igbodudu Land Fund with £100. This brought a tremendous cheer from the crowd – and an undignified frown on the face of the old Oba. 'His Highness, Oba, Apaja of Ipaja, £100,' Benjamin Benjamin dictated to a clerk who wrote down the list of promises. Then Benjamin Benjamin continued: 'Chief Obakekere of Ipaja, fifty pounds,' and he led the crowd in a big round of applause for the chief.

But the old chief wailed a denial.

'I did not say fifty pounds at all. Where am I to find fifty pounds?' he asked the crowd in all seriousness. 'Write down ten pounds against my name. When I find ten pounds I shall pay you.'

'You will pay fifty,' assured his son importantly from the crowd. 'Clerk, write down fifty pounds, and not ten for Obakekere. He is at all times a worthy next to the Oba of Ipaja.' This was greeted with wild acclamation from the crowd, led by Benjamin Benjamin. The ball of promises went round the chiefs.

'Twenty pounds? – No, I said ten,' one chief argued.

'But you first said twenty. And the clerk has already written twenty pounds!'

'He has written that?' the chief asked anxiously. 'It is not bad. Write down twenty pounds for me. Chief Eketa of Ipaja, twenty pounds. That is how you should write it in your book.'

'Chief Ekerin, twenty-five pounds,' Benjamin Benjamin announced.

Chief Eketa then cried out: 'Clerk, rub out the sum that you wrote down for me. Instead of twenty pounds write thirty . . . in all things I am the senior of the Ekerin.'

'Chief Momo of Ipaja, fifteen pounds.'

'I did not tell you fifteen. Two pounds is what I told you,' protested Chief Momo. 'And two pounds is what I am going to pay.'

'But the Clerk has written fifteen.'

'Let him rub it out. Let him write down two. If he writes down fifteen pounds he must pay it out of his own pocket. Two pounds is all I can pay.'

'I will pay you five pounds,' said one chief. 'But do not write my name in your book,' he warned.

'But, Father we must keep a record of all the money,' Benjamin Benjamin explained. 'We must keep a proper account of this fund. We first write the name. Then we write the amount promised next to the name.'

'Just do not write my name in your book, that is all. When I sell my next cocoa harvest you should ask me for five pounds.'

From the chiefs the ball of promises passed on to the educated sons and daughters of Ipaja. They were first divided on the suggestion of the railway clerk from the station from the other side of the River Niger into classes and sub-classes according to whether the patriot had secondary education or elementary education. All college-educated men, ten pounds each. The list of the college-educated ones was not very long and Benjamin Benjamin asked the Clerk to copy it from the nominal roll of the Ipaja Improvement Union. The other list was much more difficult, and Benjamin Benjamin and his group were at first in difficulty as to how to cast their net to bring in *all* the eligible fish. 'We shall ask for the cooperation of the headmasters and managers of all our schools. We shall copy from the old registers the names of all the boys and girls who have attended school since the schools were started.'

What about those who attended school in Ipaja but whose parents were not Ipaja men and women? That was a problem, particularly if the parents were Apenos. There was a vague decision that anyone with Apeno blood in him, whatever quantity, should be left out lest they admit traitors into the army.

A man in the crowd asked the Clerk to write down his name, and sixty pounds against it. This brought a tremendous cheer. Benjamin Benjamin remarked that the man must be congratulated on not limiting himself to the minimum of ten pounds which his class allowed. This comment called forth from the railway clerk from across the River Niger a promise of seventy-five pounds. His salary after eleven years of service was at that time exactly one hundred and twenty pounds a year.

Abraham Olowokere, alias Olowo, motor magnate, the Obanla-elect of Ipaja, promised eighty guineas. And Benjamin Benjamin was quick to point out that the introduction of guineas by the chief-elect showed him to be a civilized person.

CHAPTER EIGHT

The Igbodudu Land Appeal Fund got off to a good start, thanks to the energy of the Appeal Committee of which Benjamin Benjamin was the Secretary-General. They went from house to house, persuading, begging, exhorting. They went from village to village, from town to town. They went everywhere, whenever and wherever they had information that an Ipaja man was trading.

In the capital town they had meetings with the Ipaja Descendants' Union, Apeno Branch. It was one of the leading tribal unions, many of which flourished in the town. They met regularly every first Saturday in the month in the spacious parlour of their President, an Ipaja man who had made good in the shoe retail business. Where they discussed many matters of interest: appeals for scholarships from destitute Ipaja boys who implored the Union 'by the name of God' to come to their aid, as their fathers were either dead or too poor to pay their school fees; the forthcoming ceremony of the second burial of the grandmother of a member for which all members of the Union had an open invitation; the chieftaincy quarrels in their home town, Ipaja.

The Union called a special meeting to discuss the Igbodudu Land Appeal Fund and at that meeting Benjamin Benjamin was the guest of honour. 'I salute you all, patriots and comrades in the battle for the liberation of our fatherland,' he said after the President had introduced him. 'I bring to you greetings and blessings from your father, the Oba Apaja of Ipaja.'

'Long may he live!' they prayed in unison.

'I bring to you greetings from the chiefs and elders of Ipaja. And I bring to you greetings from all your people in Ipaja. They pray that God may guide your feet back home together with the wealth that you will acquire from the land of your sojourn.'

'Amen. Amen.'

'The President has told you of the purpose of the Fund, and details of what we sons of Ipaja at home have done. The enthusiasm of our fathers and brethren at home is great. The lead of our father the Oba Apaja in donating a hundred pounds is most encouraging.'

'President, I must say something now,' someone said. 'Mr Benjamin Benjamin and the Appeal Committee at home have belittled us in this Union. Since we are the premier of all the Ipaja tribal Unions we ought to have known about this matter long before now. We have a right to be consulted first, before the people at home decided the range of levies, from the chiefs down to the children. These are my words.'

'Mr Benjamin Benjamin, welcome to you,' another member said. 'Welcome to you, and I say once more: welcome to you. We thank you for all your interference in the chieftaincy affairs in Ipaja. Thank you. You are not a chief yet. You are not a kingmaker yet. Why do you not leave the Oba and the kingmakers alone to make their own decisions?'

The President ruled the last speaker out of order. 'We have not come to discuss the Obanla chieftaincy matter today,' he said. 'We have come to discuss the Igbodudu Land Appeal Fund.'

'But the chieftaincy matter is as important as the Igbodudu land. Mr Benjamin Benjamin would not consult us on these matters until he ran into trouble. When that happens he knows how to run to us. That is what I am saying, President.'

'We must not allow our personal animosities to drag us too far,' the President observed. This accusation was hotly denied by the member concerned, who rose and stalked out of the meeting.

After some confusion someone said: 'Mr President, I move that as ours is the most senior of all the Ipaja Tribal Unions, we should contribute ten thousand pounds to the Igbodudu Land Appeal Fund.'

'Motion on floor, gentlemen. Motion on floor. Any seconder?'

'I second the motion.'

'It has been moved and seconded that we in this Union donate ten thousand pounds to the Igbodudu Land Appeal Fund. Gentlemen, any amendments?'

'Amendment, Mr President. I think five thousand will do. Ten is rather heavy.'

'Amendment of five thousand pounds. Who seconds the amendment?'

'I am not seconding the amendment but I want to advise caution—'

'Mr President, I raise a point of order,' the Secretary said. 'The member cannot speak on the amendment or on the original motion until someone has seconded the amendment. After someone has seconded the amendment then the member can speak on it.'

'Does anyone second the amendment?' the President asked.

'I do,' the Secretary said, after a pause in which it looked as if nobody wanted to second the amendment. 'And members can now speak on either the amendment or on the original motion.'

'Mr President, I want us to be cautious in all we say. We must not embark upon things which we shall abandon later on. We must be careful not to put too many irons in the fire. We have a secondary school scholarship scheme. We all know that only a few members have paid anything into that Fund. We decided seven months ago to build a club house of a design and size befitting the importance of our union as the leading tribal union in the country.'

'Yes, we decided the design must be done by a registered architect.'

'All these things require money.'

The President nodded his head in agreement with the member's observation.

'And in addition to all these things we have our personal problems in our own homes. We have to feed our wives and children. We have to send our children to school, that they may not be illiterate, like ourselves . . . And school fees continue to rise. Again, Government wants us to pay higher taxes. Then, rents continue to go up. So you see, the cost of living is rising higher and higher. Yet the wicked Government is doing nothing about increasing the salaries and wages of civil servants and workers. So you see, we must be careful about what we do.'

Someone else, to the disappointment of the guest from Ipaja, supported the adviser of caution. He told his fellow Ipajas of his bitter experience in his new job. In spite of the fact that he had given the Chief Clerk a substantial amount of money as 'kola' before he secured the job, he was being threatened with dismissal every day. But he was cut short by the President who reminded his followers that if they all brought their personal problems to the meeting they would get nowhere, and they would achieve nothing for their hometown. 'I exhort you to let us put our affairs in the hand of God. And God will provide.'

The President's observation encouraged Benjamin Benjamin to speak again: 'I have listened very patiently to everything that has been said. I am very happy that God has given us such a patriotic bunch of men to lead this Union. I commend to you all the most patriotic words of the President . . . I would like to remind you all of the importance of land in the life of an individual and of a people. What was the underlying cause of the inter-tribal wars of old? Land. Why did the forces of one tribe invade the territory of another tribe? Land. That was what led one tribe to invade another. Did God Himself in the Bible not encourage the Israelites to wage war against certain neighbouring tribes? Did God Himself not promise the Israelites the lands owned by the victims of their invasion?'

He spoke confidently.

'We must all cast aside our personal problems,' he said with emphasis. 'We must think first and foremost of our dear fatherland; Ipaja first – and always. We must fight now and always for the restoration of the land that was ours and will by the grace of God and the endeavours of you good patriots soon be ours once more. Comrades, in the name of the brave warriors of Ipaja of old, for the prestige of our dear fatherland, for the benefit of future generations of Ipaja men and women, I enjoin you all to fight and fight for the restoration of the Igbodudu land.'

The meeting eventually came to the decision that the Union would raise two thousand five hundred pounds towards the Fund. It also decided on an internal levy of a minimum of twenty-five pounds per member. The President promised sixty-three pounds, called out in the more impressive denomination of guineas. The Vice-President promised forty-two pounds. Other promises ranged from twenty-five pounds to forty.

Before they left Apeno to return to Ipaja, the delegates saw a number of influential men in the capital known to have Ipaja blood in varying percentages in their veins and Ipaja interest in varying degrees in their hearts. They were the descendants of slaves who, after the abolition of the Slave Trade, had found their way from the West Indies and Brazil, and, after a few years sojourn in Freetown, had come to settle in the capital. They had brought back with them an acquisitive instinct, and had acquired wealth. They had given their sons strict but thorough education with, in many cases, university training in law and medicine in the United Kingdom. These sons had assumed positions of eminence in the political and social life of the capital of the country. Some had themselves traced their own history back to Ipaja. Others had had knowledge of their Ipaja ancestry brought to them by enthusiastic Ipajas in the capital, and had welcomed the new-found knowledge of their pedigree with qualified enthusiasm in return. Others heard of their Ipaja connexions and were indifferent. And others resented the knowledge that they originated from the less civilized interior of the country.

At the instance of the Ipaja elements in the capital, two had accepted the offer and had been honoured with honorary chieftaincy titles of Ipaja by the Oba of Ipaja. One of these had taken the chieftaincy seriously and had taken a keen interest in Ipaja affairs, informing himself of all the news of Ipaja in the local papers, and instructing his bankers to make an annual donation of twenty guineas to the Ipaja Descendants Union. The other chief was an old invalid. He was too old for his mind to grasp anything about Ipaja. He could not understand why anyone asked him to contribute any money to any funds not connected with the church which he attended very regularly in the capital every Sunday morning.

Benjamin Benjamin and his group sought the two chiefs. One directed that his life-long friend, a professional land surveyor, must be charged with the duty of surveying the land in question and instructed his secretary to write out a cheque for twenty guineas. The steward of the other honorary chief of Ipaja told the Igbodudu Land delegates that his master's doctor had ordered complete rest for him and that he must see no one whatsoever. Except his doctor, of course. And the vicar of his church.

CHAPTER NINE

At the Ipaja Native Court the Native Administration police sergeant shouted: 'Silence! Order!' He blew his whistle to emphasize this. His tattooed face showed little disappointment when the combination of shout and whistle failed to produce any result. He removed his fez and wiped off with the palm of his hand the beads of perspiration from his bald, shining head. He rubbed the seat of his blue shorts with the sweaty hand, and replaced his cap. He looked impressive and distinctive in the combination of blue shirt and shorts, red fez and red belt. 'Silence! Order!'

'It is true I slapped him, Fathers,' confessed the occupant of the dock. 'And if he dare repeat what he told me before I slapped him I will slap him again.' He was a thin man, hot-tempered, and obviously infuriated by the man he had slapped.

'Fathers, my respects to you all. May you all live long to administer justice in Ipaja before you go to join your fathers,' prayed the victim of the slapping incident. 'We were having a meeting over the Igbodudu land. We had warned that every young man must come to the meeting. When I saw Ojo going in the opposite direction I told him that he should come to the meeting. And the next I knew was a terrific slap in my face. And I saw thousands of stars of different colours.' The seer of thousands of stars of different colours raised a laugh in which the court joined.

'You lie. You always lie,' cried the man called Ojo. 'You have not told the court what you said before I slapped you.'

'I said that all well-born sons of Ipaja were going to the meeting. And that was a fact.'

'You lie. You said I was a bastard,' cried Ojo.

'All I said was that only bastards would stay away from the meeting. I did not say that you were a bastard. But the way you are behaving now before this Court leaves me in no doubt that you are not only a bastard. You are a traitor as well.'

'Fathers, you all hear him. Clerk, write it down in your book that this wretched fool calls me a bastard. And a traitor. Write it all down in your book.'

'Silence in Court!' cried the police orderly. He let out two blasts on his whistle. He shrugged. The babbling and laughing continued unabated.

'Yes, write it down in your book, Clerk,' cried the complainant. 'Write it down that I Gabriel say that Ojo is a bastard. And a traitor. And more than that. His father was a slave. And so was his father's father. And if he dare say one word more —'

'Enough!' cried the presiding judge. 'You have not shown respect for this Court. And you abuse each other as if you are in your own house. You must show respect for us. We are old men. And you must respect this Court.'

Down went Gabriel flat on his stomach, to ask for forgiveness from the Court. He was sorry. And he looked at the infuriated Ojo, and laughed. 'And Fathers, I apologize to Ojo for calling him names. But he slapped me first. And what have I done to him to deserve a slap? All I told him was that we should all go to the meeting to discuss the latest development in the Igbo-dudu Land case. After all, when we win the land back from the Apenos we shall all want building plots there. And my friend Ojo will want a big plot. I am sorry, Fathers, for what has happened.'

'You see what this Igbodudu Land Case will bring to our town – you mark my words,' observed one of the judges sagely. 'To think that these two are friends. Yet one calls the other the son of a slave. And they go on slapping one another! Mark my word. The Evil Spirit that inhabits Igbodudu is at the bottom of it all!'

'Clerk, write it down in your book that the two friends who quarrelled are reconciled. The Court has cautioned them and so discharged them,' directed the presiding judge.

'I agree. It was the work of the Evil Spirit of Igbodudu.'

'I agree.'

The next man to appear before the judges was a thin old man.

'Fathers, I beg you to reduce my tax assessment,' he said. He prostrated himself yards away from the place in the Court assigned to complainants. 'I am an old man. My children have all deserted me to go and trade in the Hausa country. I don't hear from them at all. They don't send me any money. Where can I find twelve shillings that I am told is written in this paper?' and he brought out from his pockets a much-creased piece of paper. He walked forward towards the Court Clerk. 'Twelve shillings! Clerk, where am I to find it?'

The judges whispered while the Court house babbled at the case of the old man whose sons had deserted him.

At length the presiding judge said that they all realized that the complainant was an old man and that the tax assessment should be reduced from twelve shillings to two shillings.

'I concur, the cocoa harvest is a failure this year.'

'I agree. Clerk, write down two shillings.'

'I thank you, Fathers. Your fathers in heaven support you with wisdom. May you dispense justice long. But you should not help me only half the way. When you want to save a lazy man, do you not save him completely? Do you stop at making a jumper for him? Do you not dye the jumper as well? So tell the Clerk to write not two shillings, but nothing at all. I am an old man. Too old to pay taxes. And I shall see you individually at home to pay my respects, and to thank you in proportion to the slender means of an old man. Long may you live.'

'Clerk, the man is too old to pay any tax, much too old.'

'I concur.'

'And I concur.'

'Silence! Silence!' cried the police orderly. He blew his whistle as he strained his neck to catch a glimpse of the man with plenty of money.

Abraham Olowokere, the Obanla-elect.

As he entered the Court there were repeated shouts of '*Olowo!*' and though the police orderly continued to blow his whistle and to shout 'Silence' he was enjoying with the rest of the Court the excitement of having the rich man of Ipaja in their midst.

At the entrance Olowo removed his slippers. He waved to his admirers, and walked up in pretended humility to the open space in front of the Court. There, he went down flat on his stomach in salutation before the judges. 'Long life to you all, my Fathers. Long may you live to dispense justice in this town of *Ipaja*. May the wisdom of your fathers support you.' As he rose to his feet he was greeted with shouts of '*Olowo!*'

The President succeeded in putting in a word. He wanted to know what had brought Olowokere, chief-elect, to Court. Was he suing someone to recover some debt? Was he seeking the Court's assistance to discipline some employee of his? Or did he want another wife? The President spoke as if to say: You only need to tell us what you want and you see how we get it for you.

'Fathers,' Olowo said. 'I need your help. I want you to save me from the persecution of the tax clerk. He says I am a rich man and has asked me to pay a fantastic amount of money. Thirty pounds tax! I alone. Where am I to find it?'

His question was addressed to both the judges and the Court. While the judges were still considering it, Olowo's fellow-citizens shouted from the benches 'Olowo! Olowo!' and started a lively debate on the merits of the case of the rich man asked to pay thirty pounds tax.

'Thirty pounds? If I had half the money he has I wouldn't grumble if I were asked to pay thirty pounds. In fact I'd gladly pay up to fifty pounds. These rich men do not always like to spend money.'

'But why should any one man pay so much tax? After all most people pay less than two pounds each. You go and work and make your own money.'

'If I were Olowo, I'd refuse to pay anything more than five pounds.'

'This is going to be good. I have always said that the tax clerk assesses people arbitrarily. I'd see what he will do about Olowo's assessment. He wouldn't listen to my complaint. We'll see if he dare stand against reducing Olowo's assessment.'

'Fifty pounds – it is much money,' the President commented.

'Thirty! Thirty pounds, Father. Not fifty pounds!' the Court Clerk corrected.

'Thirty pounds tax for Olowo,' muttered the President, taking the correction. 'Well, this is word,' he said looking from one colleague to another.

'How can one pay thirty pounds? One man alone!' said one of the judges.

'Your fathers in heaven support you,' cried Olowo in gratitude.

The three judges then retired to the little room that served as a chamber behind the Court House. From the room came a man known to be middleman between plaintiffs and judges. He held a whispered conversation with Olowo.

He returned to the room and after a short while the three judges came back, followed by the middleman.

'Fifty pounds is too much for one man to pay as tax,' said the President, after taking his seat.

'Thirty pounds, Father,' again corrected the Court Clerk. 'Thirty pounds.'

'What am I selling to find thirty pounds tax?' Olowo asked in pretended seriousness.

'We reduce the assessment to eight pounds,' the President

said. 'Clerk write down eight pounds for Mr Olowokere, Chief-elect.'

'Eight pounds. I concur,' said the first associate.

'Eight pounds. I agree. Clerk, write down eight pounds.'

'Olowo!' the crowd shouted in congratulations.

Late at night that same day the Apaja of Ipaja and his Elders met on the veranda of his house to deliberate over yet another serious matter of state.

'Owner of the world,' one of them began, 'do I hear that Chief Ajayi actually was present when his sons beat up your *eleyinyins*?' he asked incredulously.

'Not only was Ajayi present, he ordered the beating-up,' another explained.

'Yes,' the old Apaja sighed. 'This is my plight. My own chiefs now assault me in my own town,' he said bitterly.

'And where is Chief Ajayi himself now?' someone asked. 'He has not attended our meetings for some time.'

'No, he has not. He will not come to this either. He now goes to his friend the black District Officer at Apeno.'

'This is a great affront to our owner, our Liege Lord of Ipaja. Fellow Chiefs of Ipaja, this is word. What shall we do about it?'

'Yes, my own Chief has assaulted me – Ajayi has!' the outraged Oba of Ipaja complained bitterly. 'A man whom I myself made a chief and round whose neck I myself put the string of beads!'

'The matter is coming before your court Chief Momo. You will know how to punish Ajayi. Punish him so much that he will regret having been born. Give him the punishment that he will remember till his dying day.'

'And I'll be on the look out for him,' Momo said.

'But, Elders, aren't we overlooking one thing?' one of them said. 'When Ajayi is fined by Chief Momo in his court, will he not be angry about the fine? And if he is angry about the fine will he not take the case on appeal to the District Officer?

And do we not all know that the District Officer is his friend?' He left his colleagues to work out the implications for themselves.

'I see. I quite see the point,' Chief Momo said, disappointedly. 'And another sad thing is this: that our customs are dying out and the black White Man will say that he does not recognize this *eleyenyin* custom and will therefore not punish Ajayi.'

They all were silent for some time. How were they to get round Udo Akpan to punish this erring chief, Ajayi?

'My own chief – he assaulted me – in my own town! Elders of Ipaja, what is the world coming to? Ajayi insulted me by assaulting my *eleyinyins*. What are we going to do about it? What are we going to do to Ajayi? Are you going to let this indignity pass unavenged?'

Then Momo spoke. 'Is Ajayi not an Iwarefa? Do we need to take him to court before we punish him?'

They all looked at one another. Chief Ajayi was one of the six Iwarefas who in the unwritten constitution of Ipaja had a secret court that could try and convict a member to banishment or even to death. It was a means of getting rid of influential chiefs without subjecting them to the indignity of a public trial before the White Man came.

From that night on Chief Ajayi was a marked man.

CHAPTER TEN

Late one evening while Benjamin Benjamin and his group were combing Apeno for funds, Chief Momo hurried out of his house at Ipaja. He took with him a little boy who carried before him his umbrella and his big leather fan. He leant heavily on his stick as he walked; gout had rendered his right leg almost useless.

His progress was impeded by salutations from right and left.

'Chief, may your father in heaven support you!'

'Father, greetings on account of your age.'

He doled out appropriate responses to the greetings. 'Thank you, my son, son of the Tiger. Is your father well? – My son, get up, get up, son of the Lion, son of the Elephant, the Elephant of Ipaja, get up, get up – My daughter, is it well with your father? I have not seen him for some time.'

At the modest parsonage of St John's, Chief Momo climbed painfully the three steps that led on to the concrete veranda and tapped on the door with his walking-stick. He sat down heavily on a chair on the veranda, recovering from the tedious walk, waiting for someone to open the door.

The Reverend Josiah Olaiya himself did so, and bade his visitor welcome with great enthusiasm. A difficult chief, Momo, but a great church-goer and an admirer of the vicar. Josiah Olaiya was his constant adviser in all things both temporal and spiritual.

After the preliminary salutations were over, the old man produced a crumpled envelope from the ample pockets of his *agbada*. He explained to the clergyman that it had been brought to him by a friend of his son Adekeye, who was his trading partner at Omi Village. 'The son of my friend, who goes to the school down Apeno Road, wanted to open the letter and read it to me. But I refused. I do not trust a mere schoolboy to read to me important letters. Those boys are bad. They read to you only half the contents. The other half they cannot read. This is because their education is not much. For important letters I always come to you, Pastor. You are by far superior to schoolboys. And more experienced. All these things are important in the reading of letters. That is why I told this little boy here to carry my umbrella and my fan before me, and lead the way to your house.'

Josiah Olaiya tore open the envelope and brought out its contents. Three sheets of a notebook, very badly creased. Smudges of oil and ink blurred a word here and there. The hand itself was difficult to read. But Olaiya was used to such difficult hands, and to soiled sheets. He proceeded to read out the letter written in the vernacular.

To My Dear Father, Chief Momo, Ipaja:

It is with much gladness in my heart that I write this letter to you. And I have the hope that it will get to you in happiness and in good health, as I am here. We all here are in good health, and there is nothing wrong at all. For this and other blessings, praise with me the Lord Jehovah.

All my friends here greet you. All their wives greet you, as do all their children. They also send greetings to your wives, and all their children. My landlord greets you, together with his wives and his children. And they ask you to greet all at home, without exception.

I have heard a certain thing here that has brought sadness to me. I heard that when all the important chiefs and people at Ipaja were making promises to pay money for the new land according to their importance and seniority, you said you would pay only two pounds. I heard that chiefs of your rank promised to pay twenty, and some thirty. People here are now making fun of me. And they are making fun of my wives as well. They say I am the son of a stingy old chief. They say my wives are the wives of the son of a poor old man.

My father, you have shamed me by your action. I do not like

it. I am the Vice-President of our local branch of the Ipaja Descendants' Union here. Your action may make the other people decide to take away this honour from me. I do not like your action, Father. Can we say that God has not been generous to me? I have three wives, and when I come home at Christmas I shall marry the fourth. Is that not a sign of affluence? I have built a house at home. When God gives me the strength I will get a bricklayer to plaster the walls, and a carpenter to put glass on the windows. Only a few of my companions of the same age group have built houses. Can we say God has not done well for me?

When the Igbodudu land is divided among the important people in the town, the area of land given to each person will be in accordance with the amount of money he or his father has paid to the fund. I want sufficient land there to build a two-storey house. I shall give you your own room there. In the new big house, on the Igbodudu land.

But you shamed me by your action. You must not shame me by your action any more, Father. I want you to go to the man in charge of collecting money for the Igbodudu land and say to him that you will pay twenty-five pounds. And you should tell everyone else that you are going to pay twenty-five pounds. You should tell them that you are the father of an important person.

I want you to greet everyone at home. My words are finished. May we meet in peace. Amen. Amen. Amen.

I am,

Your true son,

Jacob Adekeye Momo
Vice-President

P.S. Father, you should read every day four verses of Psalm 102. The Catechist here is a friend of mine and he taught me how to read the Psalms and use the Book of Prayers.

Read Psalm 103 too. Read from the first verse to the end. Do not forget to read it once every day. On Sunday you should read it three times.

Jacob Ade.
Vice-President

After reading the last few words, Josiah Olaiya checked the sheets, folded them carefully and placed them in the envelope which he handed over to the old man. 'As you can see from that, Chief, your son is very well and happy,' he said to the old man.

'Pastor, I thank you very much for your kindness to me in reading to me the words from my son at Omi. I thank you very much.'

'Chief, doing that is a little thing,' the vicar said. 'Rather we should thank God who has given us the blessing to be able to read the words that have come to us from our distant ones.'

'God, I thank you, for my son who has sent this letter to me. Pastor, it is wonderful. My son sits in the village at Omi which is a very distant place from here. And there he thought of sending word to me, his father. He said to himself: "I must write to tell my father some words." Then he sat down and wrote to tell me, his father, some words. And here you have read to me his words. Without listening to him you have read out to me the thought in the mind of my son. Pastor, I thank you. And I thank the White Man. It is all a miracle. One more step, and the White Man would become God.'

There was some silence. The clergyman adjusted the wick of the hurricane lantern hanging on a nail in the wall. He stalked a mosquito that was taking liberties with his ankle, and murdered the offending insect in an explosion out of all proportion to its size.

'Pastor,' the old chief said, startled. 'You educated people are funny. Killing a mere mosquito as if you are killing an elephant! Why, why don't you let the little insect alone? How much of you can it bite to make any difference to you, Pastor?'

Josiah Olaiya was a little embarrassed at having been caught by a member of his flock at an unguarded moment. 'But Chief,' he said, 'that insect is dangerous. It carries death from one person to another.'

'Death, from one person to another?' Chief Momo said, most astonished. 'That thing, carrying death?' he said incredulously, pointing an incredulous finger at the destroyed corpse that but a moment before was inflated with a milligram of Olaiya's blood.

'Mosquitoes bite people,' the clergyman explained. The old man nodded. 'Some people have malaria.' Again the old man nodded. 'When a mosquito bites a man with malaria, it sucks malaria germs from his blood.' The old man frowned, evidence that he had started to lose the thread of understanding. 'When that mosquito bites another man it transfers the germs of malaria into the body of the other man. And that other man gets malaria. You understand, Chief?'

'Understand what, Pastor? That you will now get malaria because that thing bit you?' he again indicated with his finger the battered corpse of the mosquito. 'White Man's folly!'

Here he spat in the middle of the room.

'Pastor,' the old man said after a silence. 'I want you to tell me one thing. The White Man. He is a funny man. He is full of wisdom. Plenty of wisdom. And he is full of folly – plenty of folly. You hear my words?'

Josiah Olaiya nodded.

'My son wrote on a piece of paper a long, long way away. The paper is brought here. You were not there when the paper was written by my son. Yet you here read the words of my son from this paper. That is wisdom. It is magic. White Man's magic.'

The pastor listened, amused at the old man.

'But you see that thing there, that one carrying disease – that is White Man's folly. That is woman talk. Rubbish! Like what that lean White Farmer said about cocoa trees being sick because the trees pass disease to one another – Pastor, the white men that come to us these days do not know their work properly. The good ones have all left our country,' he said sagely, fetching his little snuff-box from the roomy pocket of his *agbada*. With the tip of the little finger of his right hand he applied a bit of the snuff first to one nostril, then to the other. He sniffed, and said: 'Pastor, why does the good white man not come to our country any more?'

'Those that we have now are also good, Chief.'

The old man shook his head in disagreement. 'You see that White Farmer, for instance,' he said, placing the snuff-box in the security of the pocket of his *agbada*. 'He did not know what he was talking about. He is too young to know. He can hardly tell maize from guinea corn on the farm, how much less tell the various species of yams from one another. Now he tells us to cut down our cocoa trees. What does he know of cocoa trees anyway? What does he know of anything on the farm? Pastor, the good white man is gone. Do not let us deceive ourselves.'

'The maize harvest this year promises to be good, Chief.' Pastor Josiah tried to divert the attention of his visitor from the subject of the bad white man and the cutting out of cocoa trees. 'Even my own little patch in my back garden has produced big cobs.'

'Yes, the maize harvest is going to be good,' the old man said. 'We thank God who gave us rain from heaven. Rain came – plenty of it. That is why we are having good maize harvest.'

Another awkward silence. Again Josiah Olaiya manipulated the wick of the hurricane lantern. He sat down.

'Pastor, there is something that worries my mind. This month is the sixth in the year, not so?'

'Yes, June.'

'You see, I promised two months ago that I would pay this month the money we pay annually in the church. My own is thirty-three shillings. That is what is written in your book after my name. But Pastor, I cannot find thirty-three shillings this month now. With there being no pods on the cocoa trees, and with the White Man threatening to cut out trees, I just cannot find any money. And Pastor, you know how much has been written in the book after my name for that case we are going to make against the Oba of Apeno and his Chiefs? Two pounds. It was going to be fifteen pounds if I had not protested. It was at last changed to two. And now you have read to me tonight the words from my son. From this paper, in my hand. They are words of anger. My son says, "Father, you shame me." But I do not want to shame my son. So I will have to pay more. I will give more than two pounds to the Clerk. Then everyone will know that I am a great chief, and my son will not be shamed any more. Pastor, I cannot find the church money this month. I want you to help me write my words in another letter to my son. Tell him that the cocoa tree bears no good pods this year. Tell him that I have no money to pay my annual due to the Pastor. Tell him that I want him to send me money to pay this. He should also send me money to pay for the Igbodudu Land case. Pastor, tell him I am an old man. When a rodent becomes old does it not suck the milk from the breast of its offspring? I am now an old man, tell my son to send me money to feed me regularly. And Pastor, tell him that I am well, but hungry. Tell him that my wives are well. Write in the letter that we are all well and happy before you write that he should send me money.'

CHAPTER ELEVEN

The District Officer was alarmed.

Four months had passed since he read to the Oba and Chiefs of Ipaja his decision that he was not going to accept the review of the tax assessments and that the original assessments must stand. Four cases that had come to him after this meeting had confirmed him in his belief that the people of Ipaja were merely running away from their civic responsibilities. He had dismissed the appeals. The disappointed appellants had gone round their fellow citizens saying that the new District Officer was not at all human in his approach to his duties and that some other means of getting him to see reason must be found.

On his part Udo Akpan had come to the conclusion that his meeting with the Oba and his Chiefs, and the fact that he had received no other appeals against assessments, had shown that he was going to take no nonsense.

He was wrong. And he was terribly alarmed when he discovered that he was wrong. The first indication of trouble came when the Native Authority Treasurer told the District Officer that there was not enough money in the Treasury to pay the month's salaries and wages. Udo Akpan called for the books at once. The paysheets showed that the Ipaja Native Authority was committed to pay the Oba and Chiefs, the Court Judges, the staff of the District Office and of the Departments of Works and Health one hundred and sixty-three pounds, five shillings and fourpence. Payment vouchers which in bold letters proclaimed that the Ipaja Native Authority was 'Dr' to seven contractors in the Native Authority Works

Department amounted to another thirty-six pounds, eight shillings. On the credit side the Treasurer's books showed ninety-seven pounds, ten shillings in the Government Treasury and one hundred and twelve pounds, three shillings in his own safe.

The tax records showed that at the date of inspection, only four and a half months before the end of the financial year, the people of Ipaja had paid in taxes exactly eighty-seven pounds, ten shillings. The total assessment was sixty-eight thousand pounds.

The District Officer looked from the books to the Treasurer, and from the Treasurer to the books.

'But how do you hope to pay your staff at the end of the month?'

'I do not know, sir.'

'You do not know. How is it that the funds nearly ran completely dry before you reported the matter?'

'But I have reported to the D.O. now.'

'You must talk some sense, man,' Udo Akpan said in unconcealed anger. 'Yes, you have reported to me, now. But suppose I had not come now, what would you have done?'

'But the D.O. usually comes before the end of the month,' the Treasurer said, exhibiting the first piece of knowledge to which he had laid claim since the District Officer started visiting the sins of the tax-gatherers and of the tax-evaders of Ipaja on him.

'Absolute rubbish. Standing instructions say that when your funds at the Treasury run below forty-five per cent of the authorized strength, you must report at once to Headquarters.'

'I do not know.'

'Just what do you know, Mister?' Udo Akpan asked in annoyance, tinged with fear.

Back at the Provincial Headquarters Udo Akpan negotiated cautiously the steep, narrow laterite road that snaked round the rocky hill on which stood the Residency building. He parked the tired Ford Prefect in the neat drive, and murmured a 'Thank you' to the garden boy who held open the door for him to come out.

'Is Master in?' he asked of the steward boy, a little lanky man with a white jumper, a white cap, and teeth badly stained with chewing kola nuts.

Master was in, and if the D.O. would care to take a seat in the veranda, the boy would tell Master, who would come down presently.

Udo Akpan preferred the excellent view of the town that was obtainable from under the shade of acacia trees at the edge of the drive, to the veranda of the Resident's dwelling house. From this vantage point he looked down on the nakedness of the town. He easily picked out the three-storey building with a red roof that belonged to the leading commercial company in that part of the country. On a sister hill in the centre of the town the red-roofed buildings of the Roman Catholic seminary showed through a plantation of trees. Here, Udo Akpan had read from files, a number of students were given their introduction to religion and philosophy before being sent to Rome to complete their studies in the priesthood. He picked out the main road through the town. From the height where he was it looked like a long narrow stream winding its way through a forest of houses and trees. He was able to pick out a few motor vehicles moving like little toy cars along the main road. His eyes rested on one that looked longer than the rest and his lips tightened in anger at the thought that it was probably one of Olowo's buses. And another picture came to his mind and blurred the pleasant picture before him – the picture of the wealthy transport owner who believed in bribes to get his tax reduced and to obtain a loan secured by properties worth nothing in security. 'Terrible, all this must stop!' he said to himself.

'Quite a pleasant view of the town from here, Akpan,' Udo was startled to hear the voice of the Resident at his side. He had not noticed when the old man walked across the drive to join him. 'I always think that building of Ahmed at the top of the hill over there thoroughly fouls the landscape. It just doesn't belong there, does it?' And without waiting for Udo's answer he went on: 'You as an Administrative Officer have a duty to stop these modern vandals from spoliation in the town as well as in the country. You had a nice tour to Ipaja, Akpan?'

Udo Akpan told the older Administrative Officer his story of non-collection of tax at Ipaja. When he had finished, the Resident said: 'Oh dear, naughty of the Apaja and his Chiefs to be bothering you with their annual problem of not wanting to pay tax. Tomorrow we send old Momodu with a dispatch to Ipaja. Today is the 21st of the month. Their total assessment is what?'

'Sixty-eight thousand pounds.'

'Sixty-eight thousand, in twelve months. That is five thousand, seven hundred a month. In eight months they ought to have collected forty-five thousand. Unless they collect twelve thousand pounds before the end of this month, and thirty thousand before the end of next month, the Oba of Ipaja and the Court Judges are to be suspended from office and their salaries not to be paid. All Native Authority works on roads and buildings must stop. The District Engineer and the Health Superintendent are not to do any work in Ipaja. Draft the letter and bring it for my signature. Come in for a drink, Akpan.'

CHAPTER TWELVE

The Apaja of Ipaja was thoroughly frightened. He sweated profusely, from both worry and the proximity of the hurricane lantern whose flame threw grotesque shadows of the Elders of Ipaja on the walls. The meeting was in the veranda of the Apaja's palace. The problem needed all the peace that the veranda could afford. With half their faces dimly lit and the other half fading into the darkness around, with their shadows performing ghostly dances on the wall as the lantern flame rose and fell, the assembly looked like a gathering of ghosts.

'This is a very serious thing, Elders of Ipaja,' the old man said. 'The White Man is angry with us. What shall we do? What shall we do?'

'But what have we done to the White Man that makes him angry with us?' one Elder asked, looking round as much of the group as he could see in the poor light. 'We must do whatever the White Man wants of us. Let us do whatever the black White Man wants us to do.'

'He wants us to pay our taxes,' the Oba said, bitterly. 'That is what is written in this paper. It was read to me by the Clerk this evening. It says that we must pay our taxes. It says that if we do not collect all the taxes, the money I receive every month must not be paid to me any more. It says that the money that you as court presidents receive every month must not be paid to you any more.'

'That is serious. It is very serious.'

'It also says that work on the construction of roads is to stop, and that contractors are not to be paid.'

'That too is serious; it is very serious,' commented the same Elder. He, apart from being a court president, was a money-lender. Non-payment of the contractors who worked on the roads meant that he would certainly lose both capital and interest on the loans he had given out.

The meeting decided that the bell-crier must go round that very night to warn the people that they must all pay their taxes and that those who failed to do so would be prosecuted and jailed.

When Benjamin Benjamin came back from another of his now regular country-wide tours in the interest of the Igbodudu Land Appeal Fund, he was dismayed to find quite a few of his friends and supporters in the dingy jail-house at Ipaja. It had been a very short process from the Court House to the jail-house, thanks to the unusual severity and extraordinary efficiency of the court president and his associates who combined duty with self-interest.

CHAPTER THIRTEEN

The situation confronting Benjamin Benjamin was indeed difficult and embarrassing, as he himself said. But he put up a stout defence when he was asked to explain himself before the Oba and his Chiefs.

'Benja-Benja,' the old Oba said. 'Why did you leave us and not come to our aid when the black White Man came? You and the Clerk are the only two who understand his language.

'You should have been here to beg him. You should have been here to tell him in his own language that we are poor people and that he should not increase our taxes, Benja-Benja.

'If only you had been here when he came, he would for your sake have granted our request. Why did you go away, Benja-Benja?'

'My Master Liege Lord of Ipaja,' Benjamin Benjamin began. 'And Fathers, I pay my respects to you, now as always. Udo Akpan, the new District Officer, is not a gentleman. If he was a gentleman, he would not have come to trouble you when I, your Political Adviser, was away. He knew that I was away on this national campaign and he chose that very time to come and worry you. That is a thing the White Man calls hitting below the belt.'

'He too is a White Man. I am quite certain of that, Benja-Benja.'

'But Fathers, Udo Akpan is no more white than you or me,' Benjamin Benjamin said. 'Only the law has given him certain powers. Apparently he is now misusing those powers.'

'But Benja-Benja,' the Oba said. 'You have not done well at all. Why did you leave us when the black White Man was coming? And Benja-Benja, where did you go?'

'My Master, I went from town to town, from village to village, for the Igbodudu Land Appeal Fund—'

'But you could have left the trip till after the black White Man's visit.'

'Fathers, I could not do that. My mission in connexion with the Igbodudu Land Appeal is very important. It is in fact much more important than the issue of tax assessment and tax appeal.'

'But the black White Man says tax collection is the most important duty we have now.'

'Tax collection is important, but not as important as the Land Appeal Fund. It is a thing that I as an educated man and all the educated sons of Ipaja at home and abroad see very clearly. I do not expect you elders to see it the same way. I only want you to trust me, and to believe me when I tell you that Udo Akpan is wrong and will suffer the consequences of his recklessness and oppression.'

The following day, at a mass meeting in the Court House presided over by Olowo, the wealthy man of Ipaja, Benjamin Benjamin whipped up the sentiments of the people against the payment of taxes.

The Elders were confused and divided. Should they now stop the tax prosecutions and leave Benjamin Benjamin to fight it out at the headquarters town? Or should they continue the very unpopular measure of convicting tax defaulters? This latter method was bringing in money. Even they were surprised that the people had so much money – and could produce it when necessary. Even if they failed to reach the target set by the Resident and the District Officer by the prescribed dates, their effort, measured not only by the amount collected but by the number of tax defaulters in gaol, might make the Resident and the District Officer relent and decide not to stop their salaries. But unrest was rife in the town. The leaders were not blaming the situation on the white administration but on the Oba and his chiefs who were now considered foolish and weak.

'Who here wants to pay heavy taxes?' Benjamin Benjamin asked, looking round the group.

No one did, and they all shouted to confirm it.

'Who here in Ipaja wants to go to the moneylender to borrow money that he may pay taxes which will later on go into the pockets of people who are in the pay of our enemy the Apenos?' he asked, again looking round the group.

No one.

'We accept the challenge of the new District Officer. We shall show him that we are the true descendants of the Ipaja warriors of old. We defeated the Apenos once before the White Man came to interfere. We shall defeat them again in whatever combination they may come, in spite of the partiality of the White Man. Udo Akpan is in the pay of the people of Apeno. Our friends in the Apeno Camp report all his movements to me. He has refused to allow the revised tax assessments because he wants to paralyse the Igbodudu Land Appeal Fund. He knows that if we have to pay heavy taxes then we will not have enough money to pay to the Fund, and so we would drop the case. But are we going to drop the case, people of Ipaja?'

No. Not at all!

'Of course we are not. The White Man has a proverb. A beautiful proverb. You know what it is?'

No, they did not. They wanted the great Benjamin Benjamin to tell them.

'Yes, I will tell you the proverb. "No one puts his hand on the plough and looks back." Again there is another proverb. "We have crossed the Rubicon." There is no going back. We Ipajas have declared war on the Apenos, and there is no going back. And if anyone stands in our way, white or black, of whatever importance, he shall be destroyed, together with the Apenos.'

Benjamin Benjamin allowed three other people to speak

before he told the crowd the implication of their decision to resist tax payment. They had to enlist the services of two eminent lawyers who would help them take the new District Officer to Court for demanding excessive taxes from them. The case was going to be bloody, but he had no doubt that right would prevail and they would vanquish both Udo Akpan and the Apenos whom he served. He was very happy to announce that for this the most popular, most generous, most patriotic chairman of the occasion had promised the sum of fifty pounds towards the Ipaja tax case. This announcement was greeted with shouts of 'Olowo! Obanla!'

Before the meeting closed promises of money to defray the expenses of the tax case reached one hundred and eighty pounds.

Six days after the tax assessment protest meeting, an article appeared in *National Affairs*, one of the leading nationalist papers published in Apeno. 'Is this progress or tyranny?' the writer asked his readers.

> Is this nation to develop along the sound lines of democracy, that wonderful system of government conceived and born in ancient Greece when the country of our present rulers was inhabited by their barbarian ancestors? Or are we to be plunged in this land into an era of darkness, of tyranny due to the wicked machinations of so-called administrative officers? Our language may appear strong, but the situation calls for strong language to condemn the persecution of the peace-loving people of Ipaja. And what is their crime? The reader will naturally want to know. That is the question that the Oba and his Elders ask themselves. That is the question the people of Ipaja ask themselves. What have they done to deserve this persecution? What crime have they committed against the administrative officers that they should be driven away from their land? That is the question they all ask.
>
> The Ipajas as a people are known to be law-abiding. Even before they conquered the Apenos and ruled the whole country before the White Man came, they were essentially men of peace. But owing to the excesses of their neighbours they were forced to

draw the sword, and to show them their supremacy in the science of war and military tactics.

Today the temper of the descendants of the brave Ipajas of old is being tried. This time the aggressors are not their traditional enemies the Apenos. At least not on the surface. The aggressors are the Administrative Officers who are asking the poor farmers to pay exorbitant taxes. Old men and women are being taxed most harshly. Tax assessments bear no relation to the proved means of income of the people. Fantastic and preposterous. Absolutely ridiculous, the taxes that infirm men and children are being called upon to pay in Ipaja.

To err is human – we all know the old adage. So we thought the Administration had made a genuine mistake and that when we pointed out their mistake to them they would thank us and make amends. But did they thank us? Did they make amends? Did they listen to the voice of reason? They did nothing of the kind.

'A democratically-elected Tax Assessment Review Committee spent long hours trying to restore the assessments to the proved means of the people. They toiled selflessly, day and night, night and day, to see that the poor people of Ipaja were not taxed out of existence. One would have thought that these Committee members would have earned the congratulations of any right-thinking authority for the way they were performing their duties, their most onerous duties. But did they get any thanks for their effort? No. Nothing of the sort. Abuse and discouragement was their reward for trying to help the old and the infirm. That was their prize for daring to say that taxes should be within the means of the people. What is more, the District Officer has accused them of dishonesty. Does anyone know anything more defamatory of character than this? Our lawyers are busy studying the libel aspect of this outrageous communication.

'You will of course want to ask who are the devils behind this piece of persecution and wickedness. We do not want to scare our readers, but we are most distressed to say that in this act of man's inhumanity to man, the black man is the persecutor of his own colour. Even if the crime of excessive taxation was hatched by a white brain, it is a black hand that wrote the instructions of persecution, it is a black tongue that accused his own colour of dishonesty. And it is a black hand that confirms the prison sentences passed on old men who find it impossible to pay the exorbitant taxes demanded of them.

We have always been in the forefront of the fight for putting Africans in positions of trust. At the appointed date all the key positions in the administration of the country must be manned by Africans. But we must be careful that we put the right people in the right positions. We must be sure that we do not send away the white serpent to replace him with the black wolf. And that is why, either by transfer or removal from office, Udo Akpan must leave.

CHAPTER FOURTEEN

The Rev. Josiah Olaiya of St John's Church, Ipaja, did not like the situation around him. That year, the pastorate was estimated to bring in five hundred and fifty pounds. Half this was to be added to the seventy-six pounds that was realized from the Harvest offerings and sales of the year before to complete the roofing of the church building. The construction had been started eleven years before, and for eleven years the work of construction had continued, very slowly. After a harvest thanksgiving, a New Year special offering, and special levies, another pillar was built, another load of timber was ordered, or part of the debt owing to the carpenter/sub-contractor (himself a member of the church) was paid off. The cocoa harvest of the previous year had made the congregation of St John's remember to give generously of the things that were God's to the furtherance of the work of God. And more. It had made the church people work out an ambitious programme for the coming year.

But now the harvest had failed. And the ambition of the Vicar of St John's to preside over that year's Harvest Thanksgiving service in the new church had vanished.

Not only had the harvest failed, the authorities were contemplating embarking upon what looked like a wholesale slaughter of cocoa trees. Himself the son of a cocoa-farmer chief, he could well appreciate the farmers' feelings.

The little money available was now being diverted to the Igbodudu Land Appeal Fund, all because Benjamin Benjamin had told the people of Ipaja his dream of reviving the former splendour and valour of Ipaja. He remembered with sadness the case of Chief Momo and the letter he had read to him from his son urging the old man to pay twenty-five pounds to the Land Appeal Fund. It was already a political issue and he who stood in the way of it was sure to have a very rough time with Benjamin Benjamin and his gang. And if he stood aside he would see money they had already earmarked for his church melting away.

Then came the tax trouble.

He had lived at Ipaja for many years and knew that the tax trouble was an annual palaver. He knew that, however low the original assessment was, the people appealed against it and had it brought down. But the new District Officer was proving to be a new broom and sweeping very clean. Too clean for his congregation.

Josiah Olaiya was personally affected by the financial misfortune of his flock. His salary had not been paid for five months. Fifteen pounds in five places does not sound much. But with his wife and a household of seven to maintain, he had to subject himself to some privations. One of the blessings of being a vicar was the generosity of the parishioners. With a bunch of bananas today, two yams tomorrow, and a basket of maize the day after, the good flock of St John's kept their vicar and his family well stocked with the produce of their farms.

It was against this background that he preached his sermon at morning service the following Sunday. He mounted reverently the six steps to the simple mahogany pulpit as the congregation sang the last verse of the pre-sermon hymn. As the last words of the last line dragged out to an end, he gave the signal with his Bible that the whole verse be repeated, leading the congregation himself in place of the ancient harmonium of uncertain temper:

Jesus, I do trust Thee,
Trust without a doubt:
'Whosoever cometh,
Thou will not cast out'.

Faithful is Thy promise,
Precious is Thy Blood —
These my soul's salvation,
Thou my Saviour God!

He invoked the Trinity in a clear but reverent voice and paused while the congregation settled itself comfortably.

He surveyed them – his usual Sunday morning crowd. More women than men, as usual. Many children: it was compulsory for them to attend church.

He read out the words of his text: 'And God spoke all these words saying, I am the Lord thy God which have brought thee out of the land of Egypt, out of the house of bondage. Thou shalt have no other gods before me. The Second Book of Moses, called Exodus. Chapter XX, Verses 1 to 3.'

He paused, once more surveying the congregation. One or two in the front row consulted a school-teacher about how to find Exodus in the Bible. The organist, himself the headmaster of the church school, was making a pencilled note of the text for tomorrow's scripture lesson with the highest form. '*Thou shalt have no other gods before me*,' the preacher repeated.

He took his audience through the familiar steps of the bondage of the Israelites in Egypt, of their terrible suffering, and of how the Lord raised up for their salvation the great Moses at a time when the Israelites had lost all hope of ever returning to the Promised Land. He described vividly the parting of the waters of the Red Sea and how Moses led his tribesmen safely across. 'With the Lord our God, all things are possible. And without Him nothing is possible,' he said. His hearers, he said, should not be surprised that he had chosen the very first of the Ten Commandments to address them that morning. It was not his intention to insult their intelligence by doubting their knowledge of the very first Commandment. No. Nothing of the sort. He only wanted to remind his congregation of the old adage: 'First things first.' They in Ipaja for some time had not been putting first things first. They had neglected the very simple injunction that the Lord the Creator of all had demanded that they should have no other gods before Him.

He was perturbed to see that his dear hearers had put before the one and only God many other gods. Not physical gods made of clay or wood, with imitation eyes and nose and mouth. These were not the only false gods in the context of his sermon but money and wealth – anything that diverted the attention of the true Christian man and Christian woman from the discipline of a true Christian life. He reminded his congregation of the futility of worrying themselves to death over the cocoa disease and the failure of the harvest. Sometimes God their Father visited His children with such trials to see how they behaved in adversity. The good Christian must not fear difficulties and trials. His Lord and Master was Himself subjected to forty days and nights of Temptation in the Wilderness. In the end He had emerged victorious. He prayed that the Lord give them strength to emerge victorious from their present plight. His message for them was that they should cast their cares on the Lord their God. 'Take no thought for your life, what ye shall eat or what ye shall drink; nor yet for your body, what ye shall put on. Is not the life more than meat and the body more than raiment? Behold the fowls of the air; for they sow not, neither do they reap, nor gather into barns; yet your heavenly Father feedeth them. Are ye not much better than they? Which of you by taking thought can add one cubit unto his stature? My fellow Christians, these words were spoken by our great Teacher in the Sermon on the Mount. Greater words of truth, greater words of consolation than these cannot be found.'

His hearers groaned under the spell of his sermon as his voice rose above the creaking of benches and the wailing of infants. He paused to mop his brow. He surveyed his congregation once more, to satisfy himself that the message was reaching deep down into their hearts. Then he continued: 'Money and wealth are not the only gods against which the Christian man is warned but any sentiments that may lead him away from his duty as a Christian. And his duty to those put in authority over him. I mention reluctantly the movement now gathering strength in Ipaja here and among Ipaja sons and daughters abroad for the collection of money to win back a piece of land that once belonged to this town. Patriotism is a most noble thing. A true Christian must show a great love and willingness to die for his fatherland. But in all we do, we must be careful as Christians that we do not create into another god the sentiment of patriotism. For before God we must have no other gods. The true Christian must ask himself the question: Have I allowed my financial obligation to the building of the Temple of the Lord to suffer because I am contributing a large amount to the Appeal Fund? If one must suffer, the Christian man must think not twice but many times to see that he does not fail in his duty to his God. The Christian man must be ready to make his choice today, in obedience to the words of the great leader Joshua to the erring sons of Israel: "Choose ye now whom ye shall serve. But as for me and my house, we shall serve the Lord".'

He dwelt at some length on the obligations of the true follower of Christ to the state. Again the duty of the Christian man was clear. St Paul, the greatest of the Apostles, enjoined everyone to obey the law and respect all those in authority over him. On the question of taxation, Christ, his royal Master, had hit the nail squarely on the head when He said in His famous words: 'Render unto Caesar the things that are Caesar's and unto God the things that are God's.'

They sang from the bottom of their hearts the hymn after the sermon:

> Christ is our corner stone,
>   On Him alone we build;
> With His true saints alone
>   The courts of heaven are fill'd;

On His great love
Our hopes we place
Of present grace
And joys above.

On them with hymns of praise
These hallow'd courts shall ring;
Our voices we will raise
The three in one to sing;
And thus proclaim
In joyful song
Both loud and long
That glorious name.

Here, gracious God, do thou
For evermore draw nigh;
Accept each faithful vow,
And mark each suppliant sigh;
In copious shower
On all who pray
Each holy day
Thy blessings pour.

Here may we gain from heaven
The grace which we implore;
And may that grace, once given,
Be with us evermore,
Until that day
When all the blest
To endless rest
Are call'd away.

Amen.

CHAPTER FIFTEEN

Benjamin Benjamin sat at his desk to compose the article in which he was going to finish the Rev. Josiah Olaiya of St John's. For he had come to regard the fight between himself and Olaiya as one that must be fought to the death. He considered Olaiya suffered from a desperate disease which only he could cure. He would let him have it in the pages of *National Affairs*.

After considering several possibles he eventually selected the title: IMPERIALISM GOES TO CHURCH. He wrote:

> Freedom of Worship is one of the reinforced concrete columns carrying the magnificent edifice we know as democracy. Knock over that column, and the whole edifice comes tumbling down the way the Temple of Dagon, the god of the Philistines, tumbled down under the superhuman strength of Samson, as recorded in the Holy Writ.

He read it over. He smiled. He was satisfied that he had opened the article splendidly, a passage that at once showed his wide range of knowledge – engineering, architecture and the Scriptures. After several scratches and crossings out he produced the next paragraph:

> We have been sounding the warning for some time now that the Imperialist Dragon now driven to the corner by the St George of Nationalism is seeking refuge in the Church. Trusting to the age-long tradition of the sanctity of the Church, the Monster is now seeking asylum in a place to which we would be the last to advocate forcible entry and attack – on one condition. That condition is this: the host must give a guarantee on behalf of his

infamous guest that the latter would not hide behind the sacredness of the Church in order to continue to commit his atrocities against the people of this country.

He consulted his Highroads Dictionary to confirm that he had spelt 'asylum' right. He replaced the dictionary on the shelf, next to Webster's *Synonyms and Antonyms*, *The Journalists' World* and *Pear's Encyclopaedia*.

This is a painful duty which we as nationalists and patriots must perform. We must bring to the notice of our countrymen that not only does the guest continue his infamy from behind the walls of hallowed grounds, but the Church is actively aiding and abetting in the crime against the realization of the objectives and the aspirations of the millions of inhabitants of this great country.

It is most sad and disheartening in the extreme to hear the most unpatriotic sermon of a certain clergyman in the town of Ipaja. One would have expected this holy man to preach to his congregation the simple texts of good living and good neighbourliness like the Great Teacher preached in the famous Sermon on the Mount. No. Not Reverend Josiah Olaiya – for we can no longer resist the temptation to mention his name. Instead of limiting himself to caring for the spiritual needs of his congregation this gentleman stood on his hind legs in the pulpit of St John's at Ipaja, on Sunday morning, the twenty-fourth of July in the year of Our Lord One thousand nine hundred and forty-nine and told his congregation to do everything that the White Administration tells them, and to ignore everything that their nationalist leaders tell them.

Of course Josiah Olaiya Esquire is entitled to his own opinion, like you or the next man is entitled to his. But if the expression of such opinion must be made at a privileged gathering, then such opinion must not be designed to lead the people astray.

We of the Ipaja Descendants Union are quite convinced that Mr Olaiya's opinion as expressed to his simple-minded congregation at Ipaja is most dangerous, and must not be left unchallenged. We say that if Josiah Olaiya, the agent of Imperialism, wishes to do politics let him wear his white collar the right way round and come out to face us. We shall accept his challenge, either on the debating platform, or in the forum of this newspaper. We shall give him battle any day, anywhere, and plenty of it. And we shall not rest till we have overthrown him and his imperialist master.

He was happy about the last bit. He would really like to see the clergyman come out to a debating contest; he was sure he would retire in confusion. He, Benjamin Benjamin, would overwhelm him with political theories and economic markets and other subjects which would be strange to the man of God. He would take him into such deep waters as material communism and African nationalism and he would see to it that his adversary was drowned in the contest. He was sure of success for he could select the long rolling words which he knew would please his audience. He knew Josiah Olaiya left the Teacher Training College many years ago, and as he seldom had occasion to address any gathering in English he would surely make many mistakes which would make his audience laugh. And Benjamin Benjamin laughed aloud at the imaginary mistakes of his adversary. He went on to complete the article:

> We must draw the attention of the Diocesan Head to the black record of this gentleman who has long outlived his usefulness in Ipaja. It remains a mystery how this man in spite of his very black record as a schoolmaster, was elevated to the clergy and got posted to the same church whose school he very nearly ruined owing to his bigotry and stupidity.
>
> We have no quarrel with the Church as such. But unless the Church gets rid of the Olaiyas in its clergy, it cannot escape the wrath to come when this nation achieves its freedom. That is why, either by transfer or retrenchment, Josiah Olaiya must go.

He read it all over again and changed one or two words. He smiled in satisfaction and proceeded to type it on his machine.

Finally he wrote a covering letter to the Editor of *National Affairs* in which he pressed for the greatest priority for the article.

It was published on the front page of the paper five days after.

CHAPTER SIXTEEN

The article against the Reverend Josiah Olaiya gave birth to four letters published in the 'Our Readers Say' column of *National Affairs*. All the four writers condemned the sermon of the unpatriotic vicar of St John's Church, Ipaja. One of them thanked the writer of the original article for having the courage to write with such 'forthrightness and inside knowledge' as he did on a subject which thousands of his misled countrymen would be afraid to approach. He congratulated the writer on exposing the wolf in a sheep's skin and wished him more power to his elbow. Another suggested that the vicar was a traitor and that if the Bishop did not immediately remove him from the church he would suggest to the congregation that they should stop going to his church. He would himself from that day on stop attending church as a protest against Josiah Olaiya.

At Ipaja itself the Reverend Josiah Olaiya saw the original article and the storm it had raised. He had received a short letter of inquiry from His Lordship the Bishop, and had sent a suitable reply pointing out that the newspaper article had been malicious and exaggerated. Apart from His Lordship's letter, the reverend gentleman knew that the storm was confined to the pages of *National Affairs*. Most of his congregation were illiterate even in the vernacular and nearly all of them in English. They did not know of the existence of *National Affairs* and lived their unsophisticated lives in Ipaja, completely unaware of the controversy in which they and their church and their vicar were the principal characters.

Benjamin Benjamin himself had been absent from Ipaja for weeks together. Immediately after the offending sermon, he had announced that he was starting on another tour in connexion with the Igbodudu Land Appeal Fund. In reality he had gone to Apeno to see the Press about Reverend Josiah Olaiya. But one night in Apeno, Benjamin Benjamin, slightly drunk, drove his car (run on the Igbodudu Land Appeal Fund) into a wall. The car was only slightly damaged, but Benjamin Benjamin's left wrist was badly cut, and he had to be taken to the hospital.

During his absence in hospital the tax assessment appeal case filed by the Ipaja Taxpayers Association against the Government came up for hearing at the magistrate's court at Ipaja. The lawyer who announced to His Worship that he was representing the Association asked for an adjournment of the case as the instructions from his clients were not yet clear and complete. A subpoena had been issued on the District Officer and so Udo Akpan had come to Ipaja that day to attend Court. The Crown Counsel had raised two points. In the first place, the case had not been properly brought before the Court for some technical reason for which he quoted legal authority. In the second place, he pointed out that there was no evidence that there was an Association officially recognized as the 'Ipaja Taxpayers' Association'. Who were they, and who was their Secretary? Where did they have their offices? What were their Articles of Formation? He asked a few more questions. The Association's lawyer apparently had no answer to this barrage of questions, as he merely implored His Worship to grant an adjournment till he received fuller instructions from his clients.

The lawyer's contact man, a huge man with a face disfigured by smallpox, explained to a group of Ipaja men outside the Court House that the laywer was due to appear at the Apeno Court that same day and would be leaving Ipaja within a few minutes. He wanted the members of the Association to know that their case was a very difficult one, as it involved tax and

Government. Any case against Government required a very brilliant lawyer. And much money. That was why Benja-Benja had come to his master in the first instance. He knew that he was the most brilliant lawyer in the country.

Not long after this the learned gentleman himself came out, impressive in his neat black suit and black shoes. His neat whiskers gave him an air of urbanity.

He asked to see the President and the Secretary of the Association. He was told they were not in town. Mr Olowokere was away to Apeno and would be back that day. Benja-Benja was away on a fund-raising tour. He too would be back soon.

'You talk too much,' one young man said. 'All you should say is that our leaders are not in. You must not say when they are coming back. After all you do not know, do you?' he asked the crowd in general.

'Don't you interrupt me. I know what I am saying.'

'Supposing you say Olowo will come today and he does not come,' the young man said. 'It means you give false information to this master here. And he is a lawyer. Do you not all see why I say we must not commit ourselves?' Several nods indicated that the group was with him. 'All we need to say is that our leaders are away from town. When they come back they will come to Apeno to see the lawyer. Is that not so?'

The lawyer smiled, urbanely. He told them that when they were ready for their case to continue they should contact him through his man who was their own townsman. He was interested in the case because he liked Ipaja people. They were gentlemen, the few of them he had known in the course of his professional career. He was sure he would not regret taking their case.

Two weeks after this, Olowo received a letter from Benjamin Benjamin, written from hospital. He said the lawyer had visited him in hospital, and they had settled the terms of the case. He had charged one hundred and fifty guineas as his fees and demanded seventy-five guineas payment in advance. He had used his influence with him to reduce the fees from one hundred and fifty to one hundred and twenty guineas. He had also paid him sixty guineas in advance. The rest to follow after the case had been won. He was of course certain the case would be won; to this end he had contacted a number of people connected with the case, from the police right up to the top – everyone that had anything to do with the case. 'Seeing' such people was of course expensive, particularly as important people were involved. He reminded the President and Treasurer that he had had to pay thirty-six pounds of the sixty-three pounds advance to the lawyer from the Igbodudu Land Appeal Account as the total money in Account Number 2 'Tax Assessment Appeal Fund' was only forty-two pounds ten shillings (paid) and one hundred and seventeen pounds ten shillings (promises). As the money required was obviously going to be much more than was originally anticipated, people must be told that they must not only pay up what they had promised but must be taxed afresh. He lamented his misfortune in having to be in a hospital bed when his presence was so vital to the success of the two projects in hand. He was, however, certain that Mr Olowokere the President and Treasurer would do all he could to rally the people round. He warned the President to keep an eye on the activities of 'certain important personalities in Ipaja who are in the pay of the Oba of Apeno'.

The story of Benjamin Benjamin's accident and his stay in hospital soon after the Olaiya sermon was badly twisted by the time it got to Ipaja. Some said he had been killed by God for misleading the people, as the respected reverend gentleman had forecast. Some said he had run away and would never come back to Ipaja. Yet others said that Udo Akpan had caught him at Apeno and that he was already in gaol.

Benjamin Benjamin's account that the tax assessment appeal lawyer was to be paid one hundred and twenty guineas and that he had already paid sixty guineas out of this was also distorted. The amount of money he had already collected was thought to be hundreds of pounds, and not forty-two pounds ten shillings as had been mentioned in his letter to Olowokere.

'Do they say that everyone is to pay another three pounds? If I pay another three pounds I alone will have paid seven pounds. All this to pay to the lawyer who will fight against the D.O. in the Court!

'And what was my original tax assessment? Six pounds fifteen shillings. I had had it reduced to two pounds, after seeing the Appeal Chiefs. But the money I am to pay to the lawyer to fight the case is more than what the D.O. wanted me to pay originally. Do you not see it that way?'

'Wonderful! I never looked at it that way.'

When next Udo Akpan visited Ipaja he met a repentant Oba and Chiefs and people. They were paying their taxes and the tax clerk reported happily that the trouble was over. Udo Akpan addressed them at the Court House. He again emphasized the needs for paying taxes, and took them over the familiar grounds of the provision of social amenities like schools and hospitals and roads. He congratulated them on having seen the truth at last, and hoped that they would from then on not allow themselves to be misled by anyone.

He then told them that Government could no longer delay action in the matter of cutting down diseased cocoa trees since the disease was continuing to spread, as they themselves had seen. Government had started the cutting out operations on farms belonging to Apeno people. There the Apeno farmers had seen reason. They had seen that Government was only helping them and so the people were themselves cooperating in fighting the terrible disease. He wanted the Ipaja people to see reason too and cooperate with Government in halting the spread of the disease before it was too late.

'Chiefs, Elders and youths of Ipaja,' the old Apaja said. 'You have heard the words of the black White Man. Very grave words has he spoken. Say out your mind. What shall we do?'

The Elder who spoke first wanted to know if the District

Officer was truly African or he was a White Man with painted skin. When someone showed impatience at his asking such a question the Elder said he had his reason, which he would explain presently. Udo Akpan, after the Clerk had interpreted the old man's question to him laughed and said, via the medium of the same functionary, that he was an African to the core like the speaker, and that there was nothing white about him. Then why had he not come round to see the old men in their houses to explain things to them in the peace and quiet of the verandas of their own houses? Did he not know that things said in the Court House always led to confusion? Did he not know that the spirit that haunted the grounds of the Court House was an evil one?

Most of the people who spoke next said that they had not understood the matter of tax assessment properly and that they had now understood, and would pay the proper assessments. On the question of the cutting out of cocoa trees they put themselves in the hand of the Administration. But they wanted compensation for the trees cut out. They also wanted the White Man to introduce another economic crop to replace cocoa. Also they wanted Government to give them pipe-borne water supply, as was to be done in Apeno.

Udo Akpan was already prepared for the demand for compensations. He announced that Government would pay three shillings for every adult tree that was cut, and one shilling and sixpence for every young tree that had not started bearing fruit.

'I am happy, very happy that you, Oba and Chiefs and people of Ipaja, have made a wise decision today. It is the best in the painful circumstances. I am glad that you have now realized that we must apply a drastic cure to a drastic disease, and that this drastic cure has not been designed by Government and imposed upon you to oppress you, as some trouble-makers have been saying.

'I am also very happy to see that you have all asked for a clean water supply scheme for Ipaja. You realize the truth of the saying that health is wealth. I will this day forward to the Development Secretary your request. Then arrangements for the necessary investigations will be started. I must, however, warn you, Oba and Chiefs and people of Ipaja, that this will take some time. Proper investigations must be made, extensive plans must be drawn. All these things have to be done before the water scheme for Ipaja can be carried out. If, therefore, you do not get the scheme completed in six months or one year, you should understand why. You should not allow mischief-makers to deceive you into thinking Government has abandoned the scheme. Oba and Chiefs and people of Ipaja, I salute you all.'

CHAPTER SEVENTEEN

In the next few months Ipaja was alive with activity of a kind different from appeal meetings for the raising of funds for litigation over land and protest meetings against the payment of tax. Waves of Government officials, white and black, invaded the town from Headquarters. Some went round the farms and subjected cocoa trees to microscopic scrutiny. Others surveyed streams in the District and asked the frightened women what seemed to be pointless questions.

'Where did the stream start to flow from – did you say that is the question the White Man has asked? I do not know where the stream starts to flow from.'

'Where the stream starts to flow from? Of course I know. It is from the fountain that originated from the tears from the eyes of the eldest daughter of the spirit that founded Ipaja. She was crying when she heard that the Apenos had cut off the head of her father. Did you ask if I can take you to the spot? Of course I cannot take you to the spot. It is in the black forest in the hills deep inside the Igbodudu. It is forbidden to enter there. For evil spirits roam about there.'

'Did you ask if this stream dries up sometimes during the dry season? Sometimes we cannot get water, but sometimes we can get water. And when we cannot get water, if we dig the sand a little, we can get water. Is that what the White Man wants?'

Sometimes other government officials came to the square in front of the Court House, sat down, debated, shook or nodded their heads, and made copious notes. They then poured out of a bottle a brown liquid which they began to drink right in the open square, unmindful of the gaze of curious people. Then they departed whence they came.

All this happened to the curiosity and admiration of the people of Ipaja. They gathered round at a respectable distance watching activities whose purpose they did not know.

At most times the indefatigable Chief Ajayi followed the officials round. He made good, here and there, the imperfections of the official interpreter in the questions and answers between the officials and the people. He elaborated on points he felt required such elaborations. 'All these things that Government wants to do will bring wonderful changes to our town here. That is why we must be careful that we do not throw away these wonderful advantages through our stubbornness. If we do not cooperate with Government, Government will take these advantages to other towns.'

On more than one occasion Chief Momo was driven round in the Medical Officer's car to the little stream a quarter of a mile away from the town. He was told that most probably the town would be supplied with clean water from that stream. The Medical Officer noted in his diary that afternoon that Chief Momo had made no comment.

But Government was otherwise happy. Udo Akpan had written in a confidential report to the Resident that the people of Ipaja had at last seen reason and were now cooperating fully with Government. He mentioned the commendable work of Chief Ajayi, who, regardless of unpopularity due to misrepresentations, had stood by Government and had tried to explain the good intentions of Government to his people. He mentioned a man called Benjamin Benjamin, 'a man who has done much to stand in the way of the Administration,' and he mentioned Chief Momo, a citadel of the old order, but happily now converted to move with changing times.

An Agricultural Assistant impressive in his khaki outfit – helmet, shirt, shorts and heavy cumbersome boots – led the special cocoa disease squad of the Department of Agriculture into operation. The people of Ipaja and the surrounding villages did not like his looks, nor his abrupt manners. He spoke a tongue different from theirs for he did not belong to their own tribe. Rumour had it that he came from Udo Akpan's town, from the wrong side of the River. Some said that he was actually Akpan's brother.

They watched the gang move from tree to tree, from farm to farm. They watched in silence and shook their heads sadly as they saw tree after tree branded with the official red paint – the sentence of death. They disliked the whole affair. Nor did the careless, unsympathetic manner of the members of the gang help matters. The people shook their heads in silence and spat in anger. But no one who mattered saw or noted their resentment.

The actual operation of cutting out was to start on Chief Ajayi's extensive plantation. He had volunteered that his farm should be the first to be host to the unwanted guests, an example for his fellow citizens that it was the best thing to do. The Agricultural Officer was going to supervise personally the cutting out in the initial stages. Work on Ajayi's farm was going to be a demonstration of how to do the actual cutting out, and how to dispose of the diseased pods in a way that they would not from their grave send death to the living and healthy trees. To this end a number of selected farmers were to meet the Agricultural Officer on Ajayi's farm.

The officer had also arranged to meet Ajayi in front of the Court House at ten and take him to the farm. But Ajayi had gone out of his way to extend the officer's generosity to Chief Momo – all calculated to help to cure Momo completely of his unbelief in new ideas.

It took a long time for Momo to get ready. The fact, then unknown to his companion, was that the old man did not trust in the safety of the contrivance that was to take them. So he had spent a long time consulting his juju about the wisdom of the journey. When Ajayi and Chief Momo eventually got to the square outside the Court House the Agricultural Officer's car was not there. A group of children and lorry boys told them that the White Farmer had come, waited a little and had driven away in the direction of Chief Ajayi's farm.

Chief Ajayi was visibly distressed. He hated being accused of unpunctuality by officials. But today he had placed Momo's companionship above punctuality and now the White Farmer had come and gone. They would have to go by lorry.

Old Momo's eyes rolled in their sockets when he heard that they were to travel in a lorry. Travelling in any kind of vehicle was not to his taste. Travelling on a passenger lorry just frightened him beyond description. He said he would walk. He would walk fast, and overtake Chief Ajayi. He said that the latter need not despise walking, as his father and father's father and that one's father's father before him had all walked with their feet before the White Man came and brought with him the motor vehicle and its troubles. And the old man was ready to set out on the one method of locomotion which had never failed him.

'Afraid to ride in a lorry, old Father?' one of the loungers in the market square said in jest. The others joined in a big laugh.

'The old man is afraid of death. Don't blame him,' another said.

'Let him die, he is old enough. And his sons will then feast the whole town for three days.'

Chief Ajayi called the wretches to order. 'This is serious matter that you are discussing lightly. And it is very wrong of you to talk of the old man the way you are now talking. If you pray to grow old before you die you must respect old age.'

Momo there and then decided that Chief Ajayi was his friend. He announced that he was not afraid of anything, including death. To prove this he said he was ready to travel in a lorry with Ajayi. 'And if death comes, I am ready,' he declared. 'Why should I be afraid?' he asked in anger. 'What has anyone else done in the world that I have not done? Have I not married wives and brought into the world several children? Have they not in their turn married wives and brought into the world many, many children? Have I not built a house? Have two of my sons not built big houses with rooms high in the air? And am I not a chief? This coral bead round my neck was given to me by the Oba himself. So why do you think I am afraid? Chief Ajayi, which of them shall we travel in?'

Which of the lorries should they travel in? That was a problem nearly as big as persuading old Momo to travel in a lorry at all! The loungers at once began to drag the old man and Ajayi in several directions. They were all lorry-boys, touts who directed passengers to particular lorries for which they were agents. For every passenger such a tout brought, he collected twopence commission from the driver.

In the lorry park, which was one part of the market square, there were some nine lorries in various stages of filling up with passengers – and a few in advanced stages of disintegration. *God First* was the lorry they came across first, an old Bedford with scars which told the tale of several accidents encountered and survived. Its agent was loud in its praise. The driver cried that it was ready to move that very instant. It looked like it, as it appeared to be already full of passengers. But someone else steered the harassed old man and his companion past *God First* towards *Safe Journey*, another Bedford, but of younger years. Chief Ajayi was about to decide on this latter truck when the driver himself told him that the owner Olowo had instructed that the lorry be taken first to a village in the opposite direction to collect some bags of palm kernels. It would be too late for their purpose.

Watch and Pray was truly ready to move off. To prove it, the driver's apprentices in dust-laden rags clambered up the lorry. The driver opened the ignition system and pressed the starter. No result. The driver switched off, then switched on, and tried the starter again. But the engine still did not start.

'You fool,' shouted the driver to one of his boys. 'What have you done with the battery?' Whereupon three boys jumped down and were joined by a crowd of sympathizers among the lorry boys to push-start *Watch and Pray*.

Chief Ajayi finally decided for *All Weather*, this time an Austin, another veteran of a war of accidents, with imperfectly mended mudguards and rickety wheels. Ajayi respected the old man's wish that he sat in the general passenger section at the back of the lorry and not in the privileged passengers' seat at the side of the lorry. Both Chief Ajayi and old Momo did not say what was in each of their minds, namely that in spite of his boasting that he did not fear death, old Momo truly feared death and did not want to die, and that he was avoiding sitting next to the driver, as the front was the most vulnerable part of the lorry in case of accident.

On four pieces of narrow mahogany planking spanning the lorry from side to side the passengers sat in great discomfort, six to a plank and with little room for movement of any part of the body. In a three feet space behind the partitioning timber that cut away the driver's cab were stacked a great many bags of palm kernels. Between the first row of passengers at the back and the tail-board of the lorry, six tins of palm oil, a goat that bleated continuously and three of the lorry boys competed for space. It was into this confusion that old Chief Momo was squeezed in the ride to Chief Ajayi's farm in *All Weather*.

The driver of *All Weather* kept his hand on the horn all the time. His progress through the town was marked by the continuous blaring of his horn, the confused flight of goats and sheep and children from the road, and a dust-storm. Both in town and outside the town he drove like the devil himself. He disobeyed all the traffic signs that warned of danger in bends or at narrow bridges or on portions of the road through villages. He could not read them anyway. Cries of caution and shouts of discomfort from the passengers at the back produced no result on the monster at the steering wheel: he couldn't hear them. Old Chief Momo was frightened beyond description.

Then it happened. Much too quickly for Chief Momo to know how, or what, it was. Consciousness came back to him, slowly, very slowly. He looked round him. The road was littered with people groaning and sighing. One or two people in khaki followed a White Man round the group. He recognized the white farmer. He moved round the unhappy group trying to bring temporary relief to those who still could benefit from such measures of first aid.

Momo saw him shake his head sadly at a human heap. He was beyond any relief. Momo scrambled to his feet as he recognized the crushed body of his companion and colleague, Chief Ajayi. He limped painfully away towards Ipaja, muttering incantations to himself. From time to time he looked back in the direction of the gruesome scene. He shook his head in painful meditation of his belief that but for the grace of his ancestral god and the power of his juju he would have been as dead as his companions whose bodies now lay at the scene of the accident.

The news of Chief Ajayi's death in such tragic circumstances shook the town of Ipaja to its ancient foundations. Men and women shook their heads ominously when they heard that the white farmer's car was involved in the accident. Later that night disturbing news spread through the town that the corpse of Chief Ajayi had been taken to the hospital at the headquarters town. Not for bringing back to life – not at all. But for the white doctor to cut into pieces, that he might find out the true cause of death. It was going to be only a mere fraction of the sturdy giant that used to be Chief Ajayi that would be returned to his sorrowing wives and children and relatives for burial. Men and women shrugged their shoulders. A most mysterious rite – in all ways damnable!

CHAPTER EIGHTEEN

The authorities were sorry about the death of Chief Joseph Ajayi. But they decided that, in the interest of the living, they must press on with their development programme for Ipaja. They had allowed the people three weeks in which to recover from the shock of the chief's death.

The gang of tree-cutters cautiously avoided Chief Ajayi's farm. For Ajayi's ghost was known to haunt his house and his farm, and would continue to hover around his possessions here on earth, from which he was so violently separated, for a number of moons before finally betaking himself to a distant country where he was not known and where he would start another span of human existence under an entirely different name.

Chief Momo's farm was next on the list after Ajayi's. In place of Joseph Ajayi's farm, then, the cutting-out squad moved into Momo's – and into trouble.

Without any formal preliminaries of an argument Momo's household set upon them. They employed a wide range of weapons. His labourers and sons and relatives wielded matchets and clubs dexterously. His wives and daughters flung smouldering wood from the fire, and drenched the invaders with water from their water pots. Dogs barked and bit the bare ankles of the enemy. Momo's infuriated mother-hen pecked the ankles of both friend and foe that stampeded her brood.

One of the two police constables in attendance had fled at the earliest indication of trouble. The remaining one blew his whistle at irregular intervals. The long blasts, however, evoked not friends of law and order, but the neighbours and comrades-in-anger of Chief Momo. They all joined in the fray – the younger men in actual combat. The scene on Momo's farm developed into miniature chaos.

'Enough, enough,' old Chief Momo cried at length, as he sat wearily on the stump of a rubber tree and surveyed the scene of destruction and disturbance. 'It is enough.' He brought out his snuff-box, opened it and applied a little bit of the stuff with the tip of the index finger of the right hand to each nostril. Ignoring the children hotly contesting possession of the Agricultural Assistant's precious helmet the old man continued: 'There must be a limit to the amount of silly talk – there must be a limit to all this woman's talk. And there must be a limit to all this cowardice, and timidity. We have reached the limit to them all, here at Ipaja . . . Today cocoa trees are sick, that is why we must cut out cocoa trees,' he said, contemptuously.

'Cut out cocoa trees – the tree of all wealth!' observed one of his neighbours.

'Tomorrow the water we drink carries disease – the White Man tells us,' old Momo continued. 'You will be surprised at how the disease of childishness and silly talk catches the most important people,' he reflected sagely. 'Take Pastor for instance. He told me that mosquitoes bring fever – ha! ha! ha!' They all joined in mocking Josiah Olaiya's silly belief about the connexion between mosquitoes and malaria which he unwisely imparted to the old chief the day he read to him his son's letter.

'I knew all along that it was all White Man's hypocrisy. Joseph Ajayi was the White Man's tool. He lived the White Man's slave. And he has died the White Man's dog.' Again he spat in disgust. 'I spoke my mind like a true Ipaja man when he and the White Farmer first introduced this lunacy about cocoa trees being sick. I spoke my mind, like a man,' he said reflectively, as if in rebuke of those who did not speak against the lunacy.

'Then they brought this other lunacy about water. They were going to bring water from the stream from the Igbodudu. As if our women and children do not now go to the very stream, as they have been doing since the first Apaja founded Ipaja.

'And who does not know that the White Farmer himself killed Joseph Ajayi? Of course he did. And then he took the dead body to the hospital at Apeno to cut it open. They said they wanted to know what killed him – after the White Farmer had himself killed him with his car, they were looking for what killed Joseph! Of course they were after Joseph's soul. That was what they were after – the soul of Joseph Ajayi, the White Man's slave and dog.'

Benjamin Benjamin had come out of hospital two days after the incident on old Chief Momo's farm. He had at once decided to hurry back to Ipaja to join forces with the old man who had had the guts to defy the Administration.

As the lorry in which he travelled entered the lorry park at Ipaja one of the many lorry touts in the park spotted him and, shouting his name, rushed after the lorry which was then drawing to a stop. 'Benja-Benja, Benja-Benja.' The name was relayed round the park. The ruffians rushed to the five-ton Austin lorry.

Benjamin Benjamin liked it very much. He adjusted his tie, he put his pipe between his lips, swung his walking-stick in a dandified manner, and alighted fussily from the lorry. He was immediately the centre of his admirers.

'I knew you would come, Benja-Benja!' one of the boys said in sheer delight. 'I knew you would.'

'Benja-Benja, the man,' another said.

'Benja-Benja, I knew you could not stay away, with so much happening around here.'

Then he proceeded to make a speech. He removed from his mouth the pipe, and waved his bowler hat with the right hand. His walking-stick hung precariously from his left wrist, which was heavily bandaged. 'Fellow patriots of Ipaja, lend me your ears. Lend me your eyes. And lend me your minds. I am happy and overjoyed to come back to you, and to join you and to lead you in taking the next step in the battle for the liberation of our fatherland.

'But for unceasing vigilance on the part of the foundation god of Ipaja, old Alagbara himself, who personally watches my going out and my coming in, I would not have been with you today. I would not have been with anyone, anywhere at all. In short I would have crossed the bourne to the land from which no traveller returns. For owing to the evil machinations of the enemy, my car – your car – had an accident in which I had a most miraculous escape.'

He replaced the bowler hat where it belonged. He brought out a dirty handkerchief, the size of a scarf, and wiped his face. He replaced the handkerchief and again removed the hat. His admirers shouted 'Benja-Benja'.

'The enemies of Ipaja were after my life and my blood. I was taken to the hospital, at Apeno, headquarters of the enemy. But, my comrades in the struggle for the liberation of Ipaja, in whatever way can you treat the Ifa oracle without its betraying its degrading association with palm kernels? Immediately I got to hospital I unearthed a plot to murder me – by poisoning. So I refused the hospital food. I also refused to drink the medicine they gave me. I pretended to drink it, but in fact I threw it away.

'Then I heard of the incident on the farm of our dearly respected elder and Chief. How single-handed and with no atom of fear in his mind he chased out from his farm the advance party of the enemy of the people. Then I asked myself: "Benjamin Benjamin, how can you call yourself a leader and Political Adviser to the Oba and Elders of Ipaja, and yet can afford to lie in a hospital bed with pretty nurses fussing round you when so much is at stake at Ipaja?" I also heard the voice of old Alagbara saying: "Benjamin Benjamin,

Benjamin Benjamin. . . . Arise, and hurry back to Ipaja. For your people have need of you."

'And so I arose, and hurried back to you. And here I am, my people. Here I am, ready to lead you, ready to die with you in our fight against the common enemy, a fight in which the old, fearless patriot Chief Momo has set a most worthy example.'

Later on that night a 'Momo Release Fund' was launched. Target: One hundred and twenty pounds.

For criminal assault on officers of Government going about their lawful duty, to wit the cutting out of diseased cocoa trees, Chief Momo of Ipaja got three months. His associates got terms ranging from nine months to three years without options of fines. The presiding magistrate had remarked that he had had compassion on the old man because of his age, and that was why he was not giving him the maximum term. But he would be failing in his duty if he did not punish him as an example to others like him who combined stubbornness with stupidity and took the law into their own hands.

'We have come many generations since both life and limb were insecure in the dark days of inter-tribal wars,' the magistrate declared. 'In this year of Our Lord 1949, every citizen should be free to go about his duty without fear or molestation. Any individual or organization that threatens to deprive the citizen of this fundamental right in a civilized society must be punished in accordance with the laws of the state.'

Amidst the wailing of his relatives and supporters he was escorted to the Black Maria outside the Court House.

But Chief Momo of Ipaja did not serve a single day of his jail sentence. On arrival at the prison gate he was found to be dead.

Government ordered a post-mortem to establish the cause of old Momo's death on his way to the jail-house. Strange tales of what really happened to the corpse went round Ipaja. One version of the story said that the corpse had been sent by aeroplane to the White Man's country where it was going to be kept in a special kind of prison for ghosts. What was therefore handed back to Momo's relatives for burial was merely a dummy that looked very much like a human corpse. Another version said that the White Man had removed certain selected organs of the body, those connected with Momo's stubbornness and manliness, and sent these in a bottle by aeroplane to the White Man's Country. Government had done this to be sure that the dead man would be truly dead, and that if and when he came back to earth under another name he would not be a menace again to Government.

What strange rites of the White Man, which, like the biblical peace of God, pass all understanding!

At the funeral ceremony at the cemetery of St John's, Ipaja, while the secret society to which old Momo belonged were performing the rites to which the uninitiated were not admitted, Benjamin Benjamin delivered his funeral oration, reading from a typewritten script a most ingenious version of the famous Lincoln's Gettysburg Address:

'Comrades-in-arms, co-patriots of Ipaja, countless generations ago when God first created man our great ancestor Alagbara brought forth on this spot a new city, conceived in liberty, nurtured in his own strength, and dedicated to the proposition that Ipaja shall be free for ever and ever.

'Now we are engaged in a great and bitter war, testing whether our great people or any people so conceived and so dedicated can long remain free. We are met on a great battlefield of this bloody war. We have come to commit to six feet of Mother Earth for her safe keeping the soul of a dearly respected leader who has here most gallantly given his life that the people of Ipaja might live in freedom. It is altogether fitting and proper that we should do this. But in a larger sense we cannot consecrate, we cannot dedicate, we cannot hallow this six feet of earth as the final resting place of old Chief Abogunde Momo. The brave men, still living, who like him will continue to fight here, there, and everywhere for the liberation of Ipaja from foreign domination, have dedicated his grave far above our poor powers to add or distract.

'The world will little note nor long remember the tears we shed here, but can never forget what he did here in Ipaja. It is for us, the living, to be here dedicated to the unfinished task which he who fought and fell here has thus far so nobly advanced. It is rather for us to be here dedicated to the great task remaining before us – that from this honoured dead we take increased devotion to that noble cause of freedom for which he gave the last full measure of devotion. That we here highly resolve that this honoured dead shall not have died in vain, that this ancient city of Ipaja under God shall have a new birth of freedom, and that government of the people of Ipaja by the people of Ipaja for the people of Ipaja shall not perish from the earth.'

In a front page article in *National Affairs* the following week Benjamin Benjamin attacked the Administration in connexion with Chief Momo's death. Under the title 'Who murdered him?' Benjamin Benjamin wrote:

> What was the cause of the death of Chief Momo of Ipaja? Did he die of natural causes? Did he take his own life to escape the indignity of a chief of Ipaja being sent to gaol? Or was he murdered? These are the questions our Administration must answer, and answer double quick.
>
> The facts are now too familiar to require recapitulation here. But one point is significant. It is this: Government, our Government, must accept responsibility for the safe keeping of Chief Momo the moment the magistrate pronounced the sentence that made him become a guest of His Majesty. If even the old man had the intention of taking his own life, Government had the responsibility of seeing to it that he did not.
>
> In fact the old Chief could not have taken his own life. We have incontrovertible evidence that the old man, like his associates in custody, was thoroughly searched before he was taken to appear

before the magistrate. In fact even his snuff-box was taken away from him.

Readers, you probably smoke a few cigarettes a day. What would you feel if without any just cause someone deprives you of your freedom to smoke? You know the agonizing craving for the stuff without which life itself appears to be drawing to a close. What was done to old Chief Momo was worse than that. He was parted from his snuff-box.

It was most certain then that after the pronouncement of the magistrate had made old Momo a prisoner, he could not be in possession of any weapon, sharp or blunt, with which he could have taken his own life. And there is evidence in abundance that he had not taken poison. He had no access to any.

That is why we again ask who killed old Chief Momo of Ipaja. Does your mind go back to that snuff-box? Do you put two and two together and arrive at four? If you do, would you say the responsibility was that of our Government? Reader, do not go too fast. Do not be in a hurry to arrive at the obvious goal lest the evil men in our Administration should take advantage of a loophole in our argument and wriggle out of responsibility for the death of a harmless old man.

All we are asking for at this stage is a Commission of Inquiry into the death – I nearly wrote 'murder' – of old Chief Momo. After we see the report of this Commission, we would like investigation made into the fine boundary region between manslaughter and murder. In the name of all that is just and fair and holy, in the name of freedom, in the name of democracy and self-determination, we ask our Administration to bring out the murderers of old Chief Abogunde Momo. They must be made to pay the supreme penalty.

Chief Momo was dead and buried, but not so the 'Momo Release Fund'. It merely became first the 'Momo Appeal Fund' and later the 'Momo Memorial Fund'. The target rose with each change of name.

CHAPTER NINETEEN

Government ordered a commission of inquiry into the fund-raising activities of Benjamin Benjamin in Ipaja. Legal representation was refused under the section of the law under which it was set up, and four disappointed lawyers had to motor back from Ipaja to Apeno after Udo Akpan resisted the proposal to have lawyers at the inquiry.

Advance notice of the Inquiry had been posted on the doors of the Court House. The Council Clerk had read to the Oba and his council of elders the letter from Apeno and explained, as far as his limited knowledge allowed, the purpose of the Inquiry.

The first witness was a sturdy farmer; he was reputed once to have threatened to cut off the head of Olowo before he became Chief Obanla for allegedly making advances to his only wife.

'You know the Igbodudu Land Appeal Fund?'

'No. I do not know it.'

'Why then are you here?'

'I come here to say that money has been taken from me.'

'Money was taken from you. Who took the money from you?'

'Who took the money from me? The big man who collected and kept all the money. He took the money from me.'

In the inexplicably stubborn way that Udo Akpan had come to identify with the people of Ipaja, the witness refused to give the name of the person to whom he had given the money. But Udo Akpan was not going to be annoyed into defeat.

'How much did you pay to the Treasurer, then?'

'Which of the times do you mean? I paid five times.'

'You paid five times!' Udo exclaimed. He regarded him with curiosity for a moment, then continued: 'How much did you pay the first time?'

'I paid five pounds at first. I borrowed twenty shillings out of that from my wife. And thirty-five shillings from my friend.'

Udo Akpan made some notes. He glanced at a side desk and assured himself that the stenographer was taking full notes of the proceedings.

'You paid five pounds on the first occasion. And how much did you pay on the second occasion?'

'I paid fifteen shillings and sixpence.'

'What was the purpose of the first payment you made?'

'It was the payment we all made that we might win back the Igbodudu land from the Apenos. Those of us who paid at least five pounds each will get a plot each free. On these new plots we shall build our new houses.'

'And now to the second payment of ten shillings and sixpence, tell me, why did you make that?'

'I don't know. They asked for it, and I paid it. And it was fifteen shillings and sixpence, not ten shillings and sixpence. Do not cut five shillings from it.'

'To whom did you pay it?'

'To the Treasurer . . . It was fifteen shillings and sixpence, not ten shillings and sixpence. Please write down fifteen shillings and sixpence in your book.' As if in response to the request of the witness Udo Akpan did scribble something on his pad.

'His name?'

'I do not know.'

Again Udo Akpan drew a blank in the matter of the name of the Treasurer. He asked the witness to stand down. He made some more notes, to supplement the notes the stenographer from Headquarters was taking.

The second witness had paid three times, not five times. He was an elderly, timid looking man. He gave the impression of not being sure whether Udo Akpan was on his side or on the side of those who collected money from him.

'What did you pay on the first occasion?'

'Five pounds. We all paid five pounds each on the first occasion.'

'What do you mean by "we all"?'

'I mean all people of the same age group and status.'

'What was the purpose of that payment, do you know?'

'It was for a plot of land in the Igbodudu.'

'Did you understand the five pounds to be the payment of the land, or for the court case for getting the land back from the Apenos?'

'It was for both. We would fight the case, and we were sure to win the case. The judge had said so. Then after winning the case each of us who contributed five pounds would get a plot of land.'

'What did you pay on the second occasion?'

'I paid three pounds.'

'What was the purpose of that?'

'I paid the three pounds to get a lawyer who would beg the District Officer to reduce the amount of tax that the Tax Clerk first wrote down after my name in his book.'

'How much did the Tax Clerk first write down against your name?'

'Eight pounds thirteen shillings.'

'Where did you get the three pounds from?'

'I borrowed it from a money-lender.'

'How much tax have you paid now?'

'I have been forced to pay the eight pounds thirteen shillings. I was in custody for five days. So my sons and wives borrowed the money and paid the tax. They did not want me to die in shame. I now want back the three pounds I paid.'

'From whom will you get the three pounds?'

'I want you to help me to get the three pounds back from them. I have asked them several times but they refused to give it back to me.'

Again Udo Akpan noted that no names had been mentioned so far. He knew he was investigating a widespread racket. But he was disappointed at the slow progress he was making.

Witness number six said that when he had paid twice and seen no results he at first refused to pay the third time.

'Did you eventually pay the third time?' Akpan asked.

'Yes, I paid it. It was thirty shillings.'

'What were you told the thirty shillings was for?'

'To make case with Government to stop the White Farmer from coming to my farm to cut down my cocoa trees. That was after Chief Momo had died. That thirty shillings appears now to be the only one of the three payments that has yielded results.'

'Why do you say that?' Akpan asked, with interest.

The old man looked at the black White Man and shrugged his shoulders at his inconvenient question. He then said: 'The thirty shillings has reached its destination. My cocoa trees have not been cut down by the workers of the White Farmer.'

'But have you seen the trees on any other farm cut down?'

'Yes, Chief Momo's. Some of the trees on his farm were cut down.'

'But that was before the collections started. That was before Momo died. Do you know anyone whose cocoa trees have been cut down since Momo died and these collections started?'

Witness understood neither the question nor the implication. Akpan's annoyance at the whole dirty affair was apparent. He sighed as he scribbled a few more notes.

Chief Olowokere and Obanla was the next witness. Udo Akpan made him sit in an arm-chair while he gave his evidence.

'You were the Treasurer for the three funds, Chief?'

'I kept some of the money.'

'Who kept the rest of the money?'

'I know of only the amount that was passed on to me. And I tell you that the amount I paid out was more than the amount that I was given.'

'How was that, Chief?' Akpan asked, genuinely wondering how that was possible.

'My chief clerk is a stupid man. When the amount that he was paying out was getting more than the amount that we had received should he not have told me, and would I not have given instructions to stop all further payments?'

'Who received the money – you or your clerk, Chief?'

'I received some myself. My clerks received some. It was all very confusing. I know so much of my own personal money has been spent on these matters. I am an unlucky man. But I don't complain. It is all in the interest of the town. So I don't complain.'

'How much do you think was paid to you in all – you and your clerks?'

'My chief clerk has the amount in his book. I don't know how much.'

'Would you know how much you paid out in all?'

'That is difficult to say. My chief clerk wrote it down in his book. But there were many payments which I forgot to tell him to write down. But what I have paid out is more than what I received, I am sure.'

'Are you sure of this, Chief?'

'I am very sure. I have spent a lot of my own personal money on these affairs pertaining to the welfare of this town. I did not put down in the accounts the money I spent entertaining lawyers and big guns from the Secretariat at Apeno.'

'If you have spent more money than you received, Chief, does this mean that at this moment you have not got any money belonging to the Appeal Committee with you?'

'That is so. They in fact owe me some money. A lot of money.'

'Are you pressing to get this back?'

'No. I am willing to forgo this for the progress and benefit of the town.'

Akpan was sceptical about the patriotism that made Chief Olowokere pay out more money than was kept with him. He took note of the point.

The next day the first witness gave evidence about the measurements of the Igbodudu land.

'You are a surveyor?'

'Yes, I am a surveyor.'

'A quantity surveyor or a land surveyor?'

Silence.

'Are you a quantity surveyor or a land surveyor?'

'I am a surveyor.'

'Do you know the difference between a quantity surveyor and a land surveyor?'

'No, I do not.'

'Are you a licensed surveyor under the Ordinance?'

'No, I am not a licensed surveyor. But my master was trained by a licensed surveyor. And I have been in business for seventeen years.' Akpan took note of the claim.

'Were you engaged to survey the Igbodudu land?'

'Yes, I was. And I surveyed it.'

'Who engaged you to do it?'

'The people of this town.'

'Did the people instruct you in a body?'

'No. Mr Benjamin Benjamin told me to do the survey.'

The Commissioner made some more notes.

'What fees did you charge?'

'I charged two hundred and fifty guineas.'

'Two hundred and fifty guineas. This sounds much. What is the basis of your charges?'

'Survey fees are charged in accordance with a scale of fees

approved by Government. They vary with the area of land to be surveyed.'

'What is the area of the land in this case?'

'The area is on the plan. I can show it to you on the plan.' He took a few steps back to a bench. From a roll of drawings he took out one which he unfolded. He then read out: 'The area is 803·29 acres.'

'Eight hundred and three acres,' the Commissioner said, scribbling.

'I said 803·29 acres, not 803 acres,' corrected the witness.

'I know it is 803·29 you said. I was rounding off the decimals. But as I see that you object, I shall put down 803·29 – to satisfy your professional objection. Are you satisfied?' Akpan asked, with a note of sarcasm in his voice.

'Yes, I am satisfied,' the witness said, betraying on his face a trace of triumph in forcing the Commissioner to put things down his way – the right way.

'Eight hundred and three acres – 803·29, I beg your pardon. And how many squares miles is that?'

Silence.

'How many square miles in 803·29 acres? How many acres make one square mile?'

'I can work it out, sir.'

'You are the Assistant Secretary-General of the Ipaja Descendants' Union?' Udo Akpan asked the next witness.

'Yes, I am assistant to Mr Benjamin Benjamin of the National Union. I am the General Secretary of the Home Branch.'

'What are your duties in connexion with the various monies that have been collected from the people?'

'I keep records in four different account books.'

'And this is one of the books?'

'Yes, this is Account No. 2.'

Account No. 2 was kept in a green hard-cover book with the words 'Tax Appeal Fund' neatly printed on the cover.

'This shows so many names. No amounts are written against the names. What does this mean?'

'It means the people have not finished paying what they promised to pay.'

'But they have paid part of what they promised to pay?'

'Yes, they have paid part of what they promised to pay. If they have not I won't write their names in the book at all.'

'But how do you know now how much each person has paid and how much remains for him to pay?'

'I do not know that. The Secretary-General himself knows that.'

'But you wrote it down. How do you get the information?'

'I do not know how he gets his own information. He keeps several notebooks. But I am not sure.'

'When Mr Benjamin Benjamin was ill in hospital you acted for him as Secretary-General?'

'Yes, I did,' said the man with obvious pride at the honour of having acted for the great man.

'And you collected some money then?'

'I collected thirty-seven pounds for Account No. 2. I handed both the money and the names to the Treasurer and reported to the Secretary-General when he came back.'

'But where in this book did you keep a record of the thirty-seven pounds?'

'Here, on this page.'

'But these are names only. Nothing here shows that these people from 170 down to 311 paid thirty-seven pounds.'

'That is because they made part payments only. When they complete their payments their names and what they pay will be written in full.'

'Where?'

'In the Secretary-General's Book.'

'Does it not strike you that this is a most odd system of keeping accounts?' Akpan asked angrily.

'The Secretary-General instructed that the accounts should be kept this way.'

Akpan next flipped through the leaves of the book.

'I see here is a page for expenditure. Quite interesting. I shall read it out.'

And the Commissioner read out the following items:

1. Preliminary expenses £63.
2. Press Propaganda £50.
3. 1st Instalment Legal Fees £50.
4. Lawyer's Travelling Expenses £12 15s. 0d.
5. Intelligence Service, 1st Instalment £80.
6. Purchase of car £120.
7. Car Allowance, five months £75.
8. Car expenses, 1st Account £23 12s. 0d.
9. Secretary-General's Out of Pocket Expenses £19 15s. 0d.
10. Intelligence Service, 2nd. Instalment £40.
11. Means £45 10s. 0d.
12. Miscellaneous expenses £13 12s. 6d.

Total up to date £593 4s. 6d.

'Total up to what date is this?' he looked up from the book.

'The date that I wrote that account of expenditure.'

'Answer my questions with some intelligence, and do not annoy me. What was the date on which you wrote the expenditure account?'

'I do not know. I forgot to write it down.'

'You do not know, you do not remember?'

'I do not know, I do not remember.'

'Do you know anything – do you remember anything about *anything*?'

Chief Olowokere the Obanla was recalled to give evidence on certain of the items of expenditure listed above.

'Chief Olowokere, in the second item of expenditure in this account kept by the Assistant Secretary-General it is said that fifty pounds was spent on Press propaganda. How was this spent? I take it this amount passed through your hand as the Treasurer?'

'Yes. That amount was spent on drinks for the newspaper people.'

'All the fifty pounds on drinks?'

'Yes, and part of it was paid to them to defray their expenses.'

'What expenses?'

'I do not know, I only keep the money. They asked me for the money and I gave it to them.'

'You mean the Secretary-General or the Assistant Secretary-General? Which of them asked you for the money?'

'Both of them. Ask them yourself.'

The Commissioner recalled the Assistant Secretary-General.

'Chief Olowo has stated that part of the fifty pounds was paid to newspaper men to defray expenses. What expenses were so defrayed?'

'Mileage allowance. Overnight expenses.'

'Were these expenses necessary?'

'They were very necessary. If the newspapermen did not get money they would not write good news about our campaign.'

'In item 5 you spent eighty pounds as the first instalment for Intelligence Service. And in item 10 you spent another forty pounds, making a total of one hundred and twenty pounds. Is this correct?'

'It is correct.'

'What are the details of this item?'

'Eighty pounds was spent in the Secretariat at Apeno at first.'

'Eighty pounds at the Secretariat at Apeno – how did you spend it?'

'We gave the European chief surveyor fifty pounds. And the Chief Clerk took thirty pounds.'

'The European chief surveyor took fifty pounds from you?' Udo Akpan repeated in astonishment. 'You gave it to him yourself?'

'No. We sent the money through the Chief Clerk. And the Chief Clerk sent it through the European's steward. The steward gave it to his master's wife. She gave it to her husband at night.'

'You did not actually give the money to the European yourself?' Udo Akpan asked reflectively, his mind registering the absolute valuelessness of the evidence on the roundabout transaction.

'How do you know that he received the money?'

'I know that he received the money. The steward told the Chief Clerk. The Chief Clerk told Mr Benjamin Benjamin. And the Secretary-General told me.'

'Which of you gave the fifty pounds to the Chief Clerk for the surveyor?'

'The Secretary-General did.'

'Were you there when the Secretary-General, Mr Benjamin Benjamin, gave fifty pounds to the Chief Clerk?' Udo Akpan asked eagerly.

'No, I was not there. If I was there the Chief Clerk would not take the money. He would call the police to arrest us.' Udo Akpan was disappointed. He showed it. Then he said. 'Do you know that it is wrong to give money to public servants the way you have yourself admitted you have done?'

'I do not know. That is how it is done in all offices.'

'Is that how it is done in all offices – is that how it is done even in my own office?'

'Yes. That is how it is done in all offices. If you don't give *kola* to the Chief Clerk and the clerks, you can never get anything done for you in any office. That is how it is done in your own office at Apeno.'

Udo Akpan paused for a long while, fighting to keep his temper. At last he said, 'Tell me, man, why did you give money to officials in the Secretariat?'

'We gave them money that they may show us the report of the first white surveyor who surveyed the Igbodudu land. It is a secret document.'

'And where is the secret document which you got from the Secretariat at Apeno?'

'It is in the Secretariat, at Apeno.'

'In the Secretariat at Apeno – I thought you bought it?'

'We were allowed to keep it for only one night. We sent it back to the Chief Clerk the following day. We had to hire a taxi and send it by a special person that it might not be late getting back to the Secretariat at Apeno.'

'Extraordinarily clever. You copied it, I imagine?'

'I think the Secretary-General copied it. I do not know.'

'Of course you do not know. You do not know anything. But you know you gave fifty pounds to a European and thirty pounds to a Chief Clerk. And you know what was the secret in the document!'

'Yes. The Secretary-General said that it shows conclusively that the Igbodudu land belonged to Ipaja and that the Apeno people paid a lot of money to the first European chief surveyor to say that the land belonged to the Apenos.'

'Astonishing!' Akpan made a few more notes.

'Now, tell me this. Just what do you mean by the word "means" in item 11. I suppose as usual, you do not know?'

'I know. We spent the money on "means".'

'Just what are "means"? That is what I want to know from you.'

'We spent the money to buy medicines and to take injections to protect ourselves from our enemy.'

'Who are your enemy?'

'The Apenos are our enemy. They are very wicked. They have powerful juju. They can make juju to kill all of us.'

'You believe in juju, of course. Did you take the medicines and injections from the doctor in the hospital at Apeno?'

'No. The hospital doctor knows nothing about these things. The white man's medicine cannot overcome juju.'

'You went then to the native doctor?'

'Yes, we went to the native doctor.'

'And you paid forty-five pounds to the native doctor for juju to protect you against the juju of the Apenos. Tell me, how do you know that that doctor gave you a stronger juju than the Apeno juju? You yourself said just now that the Apenos have strong juju?'

'I know. If the juju the native doctor gave us was not stronger than the Apeno juju, Mr Benjamin Benjamin would have died when he had motor accident at Apeno.'

CHAPTER TWENTY

The Inquiry sat for seventeen days at Ipaja, and for another six at Apeno. In all twenty-nine people testified before Udo Akpan.

He worked late one night to draft his report in his study. He wrote:

> I am satisfied beyond doubt that the sentiments of the simple people of Ipaja against the Apenos, their enemy of the former inter-tribal war days, and that their ignorance and superstitions were exploited by a handful of so-called educated people. They were persuaded to part with their money for causes which they were led to believe were in the interest of their town and community. . . .

He smoked furiously as he sought for the appropriate words to describe his findings about the Igbodudu Land Appeal Fund. He knew his report must be factual. He belonged to a service proud of its tradition of polished language irrespective of the sentiments of the writer. He did not agree with the principle but he must write his report according to form:

> The Igbodudu Land Appeal Fund is by far the most serious of the rackets. The purpose of this fund was allegedly the payment of legal expenses in some projected litigation which the people of Ipaja were starting against the people of Apeno for the restoration of the Igbodudu Land which the Ipajas claimed originally formed part of Ipaja District. It was impossible for me in the time available to find the exact amount of money collected. Apart from money collected at Ipaja itself, the collectors organized expeditions from Ipaja to all towns and villages in the country wherever men and women of Ipaja origin were known to be trading. The money so collected was never properly recorded.

> The collectors adopted a peculiar system of keeping their accounts which makes it impossible for anyone (including themselves) to discover how much anyone has contributed at any given time. My estimate from the mass of evidence before me is that an amount varying between £750 and £1,000 may have been collected in respect of this fund alone. Of this amount the treasurer, Chief Olowokere the Obanla of Ipaja, said in his evidence that he had not a penny left with him.

He chuckled as he saw the vision of Chief Olowokere rise before him, the vision of the man who was Treasurer and was unable to say how much money had been kept with him and how much he had paid out. Here was a treasurer who could not read and write but who had been elected to the office by virtue of his wealth and social status. He had had to trust to his chief clerk, himself only poorly educated and certainly unequal to the task of keeping good accounts. Where did inefficiency stop and planned dishonesty take over? He crushed the cigarette end in the ashtray as he decided not to include these sentiments. His report must be factual. He wrote one further paragraph about the Treasurer:

> The Treasurer, Chief Olowokere the Obanla, said in his evidence that an Apeno-based lawyer had charged £4,200 for the case. In his evidence the Chief Land Officer estimates that the value of the land under dispute is about £1,680 at ruling land rates in the Ipaja–Apeno area. Incidentally I understand that this lawyer refused to come and give evidence at the Inquiry for reasons which are the subject of a letter to the Attorney General in a separate file.

Lawyers! He got up from his desk and wandered aimlessly into the bedroom and back. He dared not commit to paper what he thought of this highly-regarded class of professionals, those men of the 'learned profession'! Barristers at Law and Solicitors of the Supreme Court! Advocates! He knew them well. But what he would have liked to say about them he dared not write in an official report. He sighed in disappointment as he decided that he must let the matter lie.

He poured himself a drink to deaden the anger the very thought of Benjamin Benjamin caused him. He hated the man. He wished he could have the opportunity of dealing with him the way that would hurt him most – give him the thrashing of his life. With great restraint he wrote:

> Mr Benjamin Benjamin, the Secretary-General of the Ipaja Descendants' Union, also failed to come to give evidence at the Inquiry. He no doubt was acting in accordance with the advice of the lawyer. My confidential inquiry at the office of the Attorney General as to my powers in these circumstances has not been answered yet. No doubt the experts are still looking into the legal aspects. Needless to say how disappointing and sad it is that the person who should have been key witness in the Inquiry has absented himself from the Inquiry and at the time of writing we do not see our way clear towards taking any active measure against him. I refrain from saying anything further at this stage about Mr Benjamin Benjamin, realizing as I do that a man must be presumed innocent until proved guilty.

Concerning the collections aimed at paralysing the tax effort Udo Akpan wrote with satisfaction:

> For the Tax Assessment Appeal Fund I was able to establish that some £153 had been collected. As in the Igbodudu Land collections it appears all this money has been spent in ways the collectors chose. Suffice it to say that the activities of the Tax Assessment Appeal Committee have not had the slightest effect on the assessments, and the tax drive continues to yield reasonably good results in spite of these activities.

He rose to investigate the cause of some commotion in his boys' quarters. He stood on the veranda and shone his torch light in the direction, the expanding beam of light penetrating right to the small house where his steward and his cook and their families shared two rooms. He grinned as he recognized the wailing of the youngest of the three wives of his cook. Another matrimonial palaver in the cook's establishment. He was getting tired of these quarrels and he had on more than one occasion warned the cook for his inconvenient marital arrangements. That was before the third girl joined the establishment. Udo Akpan went back to his writing. After a few alterations he produced the next paragraph about the Momo collections.

> While only a relatively small amount of money was collected in respect of the Momo Memorial Fund enough evidence was adduced to show that it appeals to a large section of the population because of their great opposition to the proposed cutting-out of diseased cocoa trees – a cause for which it is said that Chief Momo died and for which reason he is regarded as a martyr.

Two drafts of the next paragraph went into the waste-paper basket before he finally wrote one which satisfied him.

> In the scanty account of expenditure, proof of the truth or otherwise of the various items is difficult as receipts are available only in three cases, and two of these are quite inadmissible as they seem to have been prepared by persons who could have had no knowledge of what they were writing about. Of course there could be no receipt in respect of the two items of the so-called 'Intelligence Service' if it was true that such money was spent in bribing Headquarters staff to smuggle files from the office. A confidential file in the Lands Department was, it may be noted, reported missing by the Chief Forest Officer for two days during the period in question. The Chief Forest Officer wanted to make a correction to a report he had written on a recent visit to the Igbodudu Forest Reserve when it was discovered the file was gone. Two days after that the file was returned. The Chief Forest Officer is positive it was missing from its place when he first searched for it. This aspect of the Inquiry is now the subject of a Departmental Inquiry in the Land Department and the behaviour of the Assistant Chief Clerk, whose character has been under suspicion for some time, has been such as to heighten suspicion.

And Akpan concluded:

> I am satisfied that there is a case for police investigation into the money-collecting activities at Ipaja. I have accordingly made a separate report to the Commissioner of Police.

Seven months after the fund-raising activities of Benjamin Benjamin and his associates at Ipaja had been referred to the police, the law officers found that there was a case for criminal action against them. Accordingly Benjamin Benjamin and four others were arrested and charged on six different counts of conspiracy and stealing.

The case dragged on in the Magistrate's Court at Apeno for five months. At the end of it Benjamin Benjamin and his associates were discharged and acquitted. The magistrate said, 'I have not the slightest doubt in my mind that the first accused is a most evil person, and that he has been most unscrupulous in exploiting the ignorance and credulity of his own people to further his own selfish and wicked ends. I have not the slightest doubt in my mind that all the accused found no difficulty in persuading a number of the people of Ipaja and of Ipaja origin resident outside Ipaja to part with their money for causes alleged to be in their own interest as individuals and as a community. But under the Section of the Criminal Code under which the accused have been charged I cannot find them guilty, as the provisions of these sections do not cover cases of stealing and conspiracy committed in the Protectorate. Ipaja is in the Protectorate. It is therefore my painful duty to find the accused not guilty, and to discharge and acquit them. But in doing so I use the powers conferred upon me under Section 126 of Chapter Seven of the 1942 Revised Edition of the Laws of the Colony and Protectorate to express my utter condemnation of the character of the first accused. I find him to be a perfect example of the man with the proverbial half learning which is a dangerous thing. He is self-opinionated, with an extremely exaggerated idea of his own importance, and his mendacity is extraordinary. It is my considered opinion that he is a grave danger to the community in which he lives, a tragedy to the cause of education in this country, and a curse on humanity as a whole.

'I am now tired of telling the Prosecution that they must prepare their cases properly before coming to this court, or to any court. I repeat that I find the accused not guilty, not because they have committed no offence against the law but because they have been brought before me under the wrong sections of the law. If therefore there are any here within this Court or outside it who may think that the judgement of this Court is not just, I want them to know the circumstances of the judgement.'

CHAPTER TWENTY-ONE

After the jubilations outside the court's premises at Apeno, Benjamin Benjamin was carried by his supporters and admirers to the house of the National President of the Ipaja Descendants' Union. The crowd filled the old man's parlour, his only bedroom, his kitchen, his veranda and overflowed into the road outside. They all fought for the privilege of shaking hands with the hero.

After several attempts the President succeeded in getting what approximated to silence from the confusion. He then addressed the crowd. He told them that in their hour of happiness they must not forget to put first things first. He therefore wanted them all to rise with him and give thanks to the Giver of all victories. He invoked the God of Abraham, and of Isaac and Jacob. He recalled how God had been for countless years before then, how He was at that time, and would live for endless years after that time.

'Unless you the Lord buildeth the house the workers worketh in vain. You are the great Lawyer with degrees that are by far greater than the degrees of the Government lawyer – you are the One with arms of immeasurable length that rescues his sons from the gulf of danger.

'You that brought out Daniel and his associates alive from the jaws of death in the Lions' Den has today brought out your unworthy servant Benjamin Benjamin from the den of human lions.

'Were we to go down on our knees now and remain on our knees today, tomorrow and always, we still would not have been able to give you a mere fraction of the thanks and praises due to You, God Almighty, the Giver of all good things, Husband of the widow, Father of the fatherless, Lawyer of the defenceless.

'You that know the needs of our poor town Ipaja, we pray you to spare the life of this our son to continue to fight the cause of our town. Other towns can boast of several doctors and lawyers and engineers. But because of the bad work of our enemy we have only this one son. Please God, spare him for us. Father in heaven, spare Mr Benjamin Benjamin, and bless our town Ipaja.

'We are foreigners here in Apeno. Please, Father, guide our feet and our eyes back to our hometown Ipaja. If you see any of us that is being corrupted by influences here in Apeno to forget his father and his mother in Ipaja, God, do your work and show them back home. If any of our sons now or at any time stray away from the narrow path that leads to the gates of Life and go after the Delilahs of the Philistines of Apeno for the satisfaction of the sinful desires of the flesh, God Almighty, Father in heaven, ring the bell of Ipaja in their ears—

'And God the Father . . . And God the Son . . . And God the Holy Ghost – please overlook the shortcomings of us your children, members of this Union, now assembled to give thanks to you for the wonderful victory you have given our brother over his accusers and for delivering him from the gates of the jail-house. The rulers of this land conspired to extinguish the beacon by which the feet of our Union in Ipaja are guided. But like all earthly rulers their kingdom is of this earth, and shall perish here on earth. That, Father of all mercies, is why we now pray in one voice, with reverence, and say:

'Thy Kingdom Come O God,
Thy rule on earth begin,
Arise O morning Star,
Arise and never Set over Ipaja.'

At Ipaja itself a hero's welcome was awaiting Benjamin

Benjamin. He spent the night at Apeno and came home to Ipaja the following day. Word had gone ahead of him to Ipaja that not only had he won the case against Government but that the court had actually decided that the black White Man be removed from their District, that the people of Ipaja be exempted from the payment of tax for the next five years, and in recognition of his bravery and cleverness, Benjamin Benjamin was to be made the Prime Minister of the country forthwith. The judge, it was said, had already written the letter of the appointment of the hero as Prime Minister, and the Governor was already flying to the White Man's country to tell them the news.

The news had plenty of time to spread in Ipaja and the villages and hamlets and to assume various shades before Benjamin Benjamin reached the stream half a mile before the gates of Ipaja. There a huge crowd had formed, awaiting his arrival.

There were three private cars and one lorry to supplement the taxi in which Benjamin Benjamin had travelled from Apeno. He and the President of the Ipaja Improvement Union who had travelled with him from Apeno rode at the back of the most imposing of the five vehicles, an Opel Kapitan saloon which was on test preparatory to being purchased by the Secretary-General 'for the advancement of the cause of Ipaja'. The important people distributed themselves round the remaining three cars, while the strong ones among the rank and file of supporters fought their way into the lorry. Then, led by a long line of cyclists, pedestrians and drummers, the procession wended its way into the town.

Men and women and children came to their verandas to watch and to shout. Several joined the procession to participate in what was going to be a national festival.

One of the lorry boys, from whom Benjamin Benjamin's main support came, sat on the off-side front mudguard of the lorry and blew a whistle continuously, and made signs to the crowd of onlookers that they should join and follow the procession to the lorry park where there was going to be a big rally. The lorry and the cars hooted and the cyclists rang their bells as the procession wended its way along the narrow laterite road to the town centre.

A large crowd had already assembled at the lorry park when the procession reached it. The noise in the Ipaja town centre was incredible: shouts of welcome, hooting of cars, jingling of cycle bells, all merged into an appalling noise to greet Benjamin Benjamin.

In times past he had himself directed affairs on such occasions. He knew when to appeal for order and get it. There was no recognized master of ceremonies now and the uncoordinated efforts of two lorry touts who were competing with each other for recognition went unheeded. Benjamin Benjamin enjoyed the confusion. Only he could control such a situation. He wanted enough time to elapse and give the people the chance of seeing that.

Then he climbed out of the car with great dignity. He removed from his mouth the long pipe which he had all the time carried in his mouth. Holding the pipe loosely in his left hand, he removed his pair of glasses from his nose and screwed his face into an ugly contortion. He quickly replaced the glasses and smiled: all this calculated to give the impression that in his labours for the redemption of the fatherland his sight had become so impaired that he could not see a thing without the glasses.

He next held up his pipe. Instead of silence there came a fresh burst of shouts. He laughed – and they all laughed and shouted his name.

At last he was able to speak. 'Fathers, Mothers; Elders, Youths. Fellow patriots of Ipaja – my comrades-in-arms. I salute you all for your great victory in this great battle of right against might. The victory is yours. I am no more than the unworthy medium through whom the founder of Ipaja has brought it to you.' He stopped. His words did not fail to bring the applause he intended. He continued: 'When I see you like this, solidly behind me, demonstrating in no uncertain terms your stand for freedom and right and your demand for the restoration of the land, the fertile land that your fathers owned before you but which was stolen by the White Man and given to your enemy the Apenos – I weep for joy.'

He wept. He brought out a silk handkerchief and wiped the tears from his eyes. It produced the desired effect.

'It is already eighteen years when I was a schoolboy here in this town of my forbears that I swore to dedicate my life to the service of my native town – Ipaja. It was then that I swore to right the wrongs that the White Man and the agents of the White Man had committed against our native land.

'When I was away in your interest, Udo Akpan, who is called a District Officer, and his agents tried to deceive you into believing that I had run away from you. They nearly succeeded in their evil machinations by shaking your loyalty and your belief in my integrity and steadfastness of purpose . . .

'Then came the incident of the brutal murder of our dearly respected Elder, Chief Momo the Brave. He was murdered by Government after he had shown that he would not stick that nonsense of Government saying that to make cocoa trees produce more you first have to kill the trees! Who ever heard greater nonsense? Single-handed old Chief Momo thrashed the agents of the black White Man off his farm. I and the Momo Defence Committee were still busy arranging his defence when – when – when they – murdered – him—' He again wiped the tears from his cheek.

'But Momo is not dead. And the Momo case is far from being buried. For I have arranged with a King's Counsel from England to represent the family of the late Chief in particular and the Ipaja community in general in the great case of damages which we are instituting against Udo Akpan and against the Government severally and jointly.

'I now request everyone here, man and woman, young and old, to observe with me two minutes silence in memory of the brave Chief Momo – victim of brutal murder.'

After the two minutes silence he resumed, 'Government thought that by persecuting me I would give up the fight in your cause. They set up a Commission of Inquiry. Why, they said that I have been collecting money from you. I ask you, my people, what is their concern there? Is it their own money? I ask again, does the money belong to Government? Why does Government not remove the beam in its own eye? Let Government first account for the hundred million pounds which was sent to the people of Ipaja by the King of England but which has now been stolen and divided by the officials of this corrupt Government.

'Yes, they are very corrupt indeed. I did not tell you this. You won't believe it. It is fantastic. Before the Inquiry Government sent to me a man with ten thousand pounds, to beg me to give up my activities. Ten thousand pounds. They want me to sell you to them for the sum of ten thousand pounds. They want me to become rich and you to become slaves. And I refused. I refused because I am a true-born Ipaja man. And as a true-born Ipaja man, I am a man of honour.

'When they knew they couldn't bribe me they started the Inquiry, the sham Inquiry. Then from persecution they went to prosecution. And in spite of persecution and prosecution – I am today free. I am declared free by the magistrate.'

'Benja-Benja!'

'But fathers and mothers and co-patriots of Ipaja, we must not allow our great victory over the enemy in the law-courts to lull us into a false sense of security. Elders and youths of Ipaja, men and women of Ipaja, we have won only one battle in the fight for freedom. We must not mistake this victory for the end of the struggle. This is not the end. This is not even the beginning of the end. But in some measure we may say that it is the end of the beginning. . . .

'We shall from now on take the initiative. We shall from now on dictate the pace of the war, total war, war to the finish.

'And when the time comes for the final assault we shall fight with all kinds of weapons, with all our resources at all hours of the day and all days of the week. Our battle cry then shall be, "One man, one matchet, One woman, one stick, One child, one stone!'"

'One man, one matchet—' they repeated after him.

'One woman, one stick!' he cried.

'One woman, one stick,' they repeated, even louder.

'One child, one stone!' he cried like one possessed.

'One child, one stone,' they screamed in frenzy.

CHAPTER TWENTY-TWO

A few days after at Apeno the Rev. Josiah Olaiya surveyed the little of the inside of the sitting-room that he could see from the porch, and wondered that an African like himself could live in such splendour. The steward had hurried out to meet him in the porch and, after inquiring who he was had told him that Master was at that time busy speaking to the Resident on the telephone and that he would go to announce him as soon as he finished on the phone. He looked round the gardens, the spacious plot of land on the hill in which the bungalow, big as it was, was swallowed up like a hut in a farm. He noticed how well trimmed the grass was. He saw a gardener watering the flowers. At that moment the gardener put down the watering can and took the hand roller. He began to pull it up and down the circular lawn that formed the island of the drive in front of the house. The Rev. Josiah Olaiya opened his mouth at the discovery – it was the rolling of the lawn this way that made it so smooth, and so pretty.

'Master says you should sit down inside. He will come out soon.'

Inside he was dazzled further by the shining furniture – the four cushioned arm-chairs, the cushioned settee, the tables and stools, the curtains on the doors and the blinds on the windows. The floor was covered with a big red carpet. He looked across the sitting-room into the dining-room. A big dining table round which were ranged six chairs. A white, big frigidaire. He knew that, and its purpose. He had seen one and had been served with a very diluted drink of lemon juice from a bottle taken from one by the principal of the Missionary Teacher Training College after he had conducted a Sunday morning service at the College.

'I'm so sorry – so very sorry to have kept you waiting, sir,' Udo Akpan apologized, bursting out from the bedroom. Through the door Josiah Olaiya caught a glimpse of the big double bed. 'It has been a long conversation with the Resident. Very important matter, as usual.'

'Good afternoon, sir,' the visitor said, shaking the hand his host offered.

'You embarrass me when you say "sir" to me, Rev. Olaiya,' the young man muttered. 'Please sit down, and make yourself quite comfortable. What will you have to drink? Steward, bring drinks for two masters.'

'Thank you, sir, thank you. I thank you for welcoming me in your house, D.O. And I am happy that I have lived to see this day when a man of my own colour is the District Officer, living in this great house. I give praise to God Almighty that He has made me live to this day when I, a lowly parish priest Josiah Olaiya, without any university degree, without being a doctor or a lawyer, without being an engineer, but a lowly parish priest, have knocked at the door of this house and have not been driven away by the steward or by the dog.'

'You will always be welcome in my house, sir. . . . I am sorry, sir, that my wife is away. She would have made you fine chop. Beer, or whisky and soda? Or gin and tonic?'

The visitor's confusion was apparent. He looked at the wide range of bottles on the trolley. He did not recognize the names that Udo Akpan rolled out. 'Orange squash, sir, orange squash. That is what I want, D.O.,' he said fixing his eye on the one label not unfamiliar to him.

'Orange squash – that is a woman's drink, Pastor. I'll mix you a cocktail. There is nothing wrong with a little of the stuff – for your stomach's sake. Don't say I don't know my bible, eh?'

• • • • •

Udo Akpan considered what the Rev. Olaiya said was the purpose of his visit for a long time without speaking. He lit a cigarette and took one long pull from it. He shook his head. 'I am certain it is absolutely untrue, Pastor, absolutely.'

'The story has spread round the town, D.O. I heard it from the sexton first. Then Chief Obanla confirmed it when he and the Assistant secretary came to my house to discuss details of the Thanksgiving Service. "Thanksgiving Service for victory over our enemy, and for Government deciding that we should not cut down cocoa trees any more," he said. When I asked him who told him that Government had taken the decision he said it was Benjamin Benjamin, and that it was true.'

The visitor saw the spasm of hatred that flickered across the D.O.'s face at the mention of that name. 'I know that all the time Benjamin Benjamin tells lies. But they all believe him. I know it is not true. But I thought that I should see you myself to check up the facts in connexion with this particular case. It is very important. And that is why I have come. Is it true, D.O., or is it not true?'

Again Udo Akpan pondered the question. He paced up and down the sitting-room. Anxiety lit up the face of the visitor. Was the D.O. going to change his mind, and say after all that it was true Government had decided not to proceed with the cutting down of cocoa trees? That would mean that Benjamin Benjamin was right. That would mean another victory for his old adversary; another step on the downward path to unimportance and oblivion. In the priestly heart of Josiah Olaiya two conflicting desires fought for mastery: one wanted Benjamin Benjamin proved wrong and condemned, the other wanted the alleged Government decision to be true for the sake of his parishioners whose prosperity depended on cocoa.

'Rev. Olaiya, you see how I hesitated before saying yes or no. This is not because I have any doubt in my mind about it. I'm absolutely certain Government has taken no such decision. I have hesitated that I may give myself time to think out what may be the possible cause of this new falsehood. Benjamin

Benjamin is a dangerous man, Pastor. He is. I do not want to be content with just knowing that he is lying, but I want to be sure that when next I catch him I allow no loophole. All I can say now is that there is no change in Government policy.'

He removed the cigarette from his mouth, and crushed it thoughtfully in the porcelain ashtray. 'I have regarded you as my confidant in this District, Pastor. And I am glad to say you have given me no cause to regret it. I was at the capital yesterday. I had a long discussion with the Commissioner of Police. I went with the Assistant Director of Agriculture. On the 25th of this month a special contingent of police will arrive in this District. Three days after that the special cutting-down gang of the Agricultural Department will arrive to recommence operations. Those are the facts, Pastor.'

Both men were silent for some time. The younger man resumed his smoking, and poured out another drink for his visitor.

The visitor drained the second glass, and appeared to thirst for more. Udo Akpan reflected that the old boy was not as much of a novice as he had been led to assume. He poured out a third glass.

'I thank you very much for your great hospitality, sir. I thank you very much.' The priest rose to take his leave. 'I must be going now.' He took his hat from the top of the lampstand and screwed it on his head.

'But you must have another glass, Pastor, I insist.'

'No, I must not, D.O. I must not. A little for my stomach's sake, yes. But too much is not becoming of a clergyman. . . . I thank you for your great hospitality. There is joy in my heart, and praise on my lips to God Almighty that has made me live to see this day when I can sit down in the house of the District Officer and partake of drinks with him. . . . The European D.O., who was here three years ago had a dog that was as big as a bull, and no African dared come within miles of this house. For all these things, D.O., we thank Him who is the Giver of all good things.'

Udo Akpan drove his visitor to the lorry park in his Ford Prefect. On the way the older man leant back and dozed off in the comfort of the car. Akpan thought it was best to let the cocktail take its course. Its effect would wear off before they got to the lorry park, he hoped. He occupied his own mind with the problems of his administration, the difficulties created by Benjamin Benjamin, the inefficiency of everyone that had anything to do with the case that had ended in a fiasco.

Lounging in his white trousers and polo shirt after supper the day after Josiah Olaiya's visit, Udo Akpan began to go through the day's papers. They had taken the whole day arriving from the capital city where they were published. He read the big type, front page, headline in *National Affairs*: REPRIEVE FOR COCOA. Under a subtitle he read: VICTORY FOR THE PEOPLE'S STAND. He read with a mixture of excitement and anxiety:

> We this morning have the honour of bringing to the fifty million inhabitants of this great land in general and the estimated six million cocoa farmers in particular good tidings. Their cocoa trees, the source of the wealth of the farmers and the main source of the revenue of this great country are now safe from the evil conspiracy of colonial imperialism. Our Government has now been forced to abandon the wicked policy of mass extermination of cocoa plantations. Whitehall has at last seen reason, and instructed its off-shoot in this country to abandon the scheme, the wicked scheme, the shameless conspiracy against the poor cocoa farmer.
>
> We of this paper, true to our motto of service to the nation without hope of reward or praise or recognition, rejoice with the nation in this great victory. We do not want to recount the many milestones in the bloody struggle that has led to this, the greatest of all victories against imperialism. Every one of those milestones carries evidence of the death-dealing editorial bullets of *National Affairs*. We are happy that our bullets have pierced the heart of the monster. We are happy that we have been counted worthy to have taken a leading part in the bloody battle that has led to this spectacular victory.
>
> In this hour of victory we warn our people of this great land to be on their guard against saboteurs. We warn them not to listen to

people however highly they may be placed, who will try to mislead them by discrediting our statement. We must make allowances for the like of them in all communities – in all walks of life, the house of God not excluded. When they come to you and say to you: 'Farmer, there is no known cure for your cocoa disease. You must therefore cut down all diseased trees' you should tell them to go to hell, and if they continue to pester your life, you should show them the way to hell. . . . We have a team of defence lawyers retained by us in our well-prepared scheme to put the last nail in the coffin of the imperialist dragon.

Of course it wasn't true, Udo Akpan easily convinced himself. Absolute fabrication from beginning to end. Apparently written by Benjamin Benjamin himself. There was no doubt that this was the same story that the village folk in Ipaja had heard and had started the silly talk that was the subject of Josiah Olaiya's visit the day before.

He glanced through the other pages. He read the headlines: NATIONALIST PARTY PRESSES FOR IMMEDIATE AFRICAN MAJORITY IN LEGISLATURE; EXPERTS ANNOUNCE RICH OILFINDS IN THE COUNTRY; COUNTRY'S TRADE BUOYANT; OCTOGENARIAN'S DEATH IS MOURNED BY ALL NATIONALISTS. His attention was arrested by one headline on the last page: FAMOUS NATIONALIST ARRIVES IN CAPITAL FROM PROTECTORATE. He read the news under the headline:

Among the great personalities who arrived in the capital yesterday was Mr Benjamin Benjamin, the foremost champion of the cocoa farmers and of the anti-tax movement in the Ipaja District. Mr Benjamin Benjamin has just been discharged and acquitted in the famous Rex *vs* Benjamin Benjamin and Others case. When interviewed by our reporter at his hotel yesterday the great nationalist refused to disclose the nature of his visit to the capital. Usually well-informed sources however confirm what we already know, that Mr Benjamin Benjamin's visit is not unconnected with the new development in the cocoa disease controversy about which there is an editorial on the first page of this paper today. Whatever the nature of his business, we welcome this great son of the people to the capital, and assure him that we of this paper are as ever before on his side in his struggle for the total destruction of the enemy.

His steward noticed that at table that night Akpan did not eat much and was harder to please than usual. The boy shook his head and muttered to himself.

Akpan went to bed but could not sleep for a long time. He kept on thinking of the possibility of the impossible happening. Supposing what was in the papers was true? Supposing Benjamin Benjamin and the paper were right and he was wrong. Supposing Government had truly decided that cocoa trees would no longer be cut down. Who after all was Government? He was Government in Apeno and Ipaja. And in the capital city – why, he was in the place only six days before then. He tried to read himself to sleep, assisted by three large whisky-and-sodas.

At cockcrow of the morning following the night on which Udo Akpan had had to drink and read himself to sleep an unusual caller was received by His Highness the Oba of Ipaja. The Oba was not unused to people coming to see him so early in the morning. By tradition a particular chief must be the first human being that he must set eyes upon every day, and this chief regularly called to 'wake' the Oba long before cockcrow every day. Even though things had changed a great deal and only few Ipaja citizens still brought their troubles to the Oba, such of them that still came usually chose to come very early in the morning – when the ears of the Oba were ready to listen to their complaints and his mind still fresh to give the best judgement. But the Oba himself was surprised, when he learnt that his caller was the Rev. Josiah Olaiya of St John's. He decided that what brought him must be very important. After a whispered consultation with an earlier caller in his bedroom, he directed that the priest be shown into one of the two rooms opening out into the veranda. He girded on his velvet cloth, and went to join his visitor, taking with him a bush lantern.

Josiah Olaiya rose in salutation as the old Oba put down the lantern, and closed the door behind him. He made the usual expressions of long life to the Oba. He told the Oba that he knew that he must have been wondering why he had called to see him so early in the morning. The Oba was indeed wondering that, but he kept dignified silence for his visitor to say why he had broken his usual boycott of the palace and called so early in the morning. The Oba thought that perhaps he had come to preach that he should cease practising the heathen rites connected with the many festivals of Ipaja, but Olaiya reassured him that, although he would be the happiest of men if these things for which he had been praying tirelessly for many years should come to pass, that was not the purpose of his coming. As a servant of God and as an educated African it was his duty to inform the Oba and his people that they had permitted themselves to be misled by those who were only making use of them for their own selfish ends. He had known this for a long time, but he had refrained from coming out into the open, as the people he mentioned hated him and would accuse him of all sorts of things. He did not worry about the bad things they wrote about him in the papers, but as a priest he had to be careful about what he did.

He could, however, no longer resist coming to talk to the Oba. They should not believe the story that was gaining ground that the British Government from London had given direct instructions that Mr Benjamin Benjamin be made Prime Minister and that the cutting down of cocoa trees should be stopped. He tried to explain to the Oba the preliminary requirements of a person going through elections before he can get into the National Assembly, before he can be made the Prime Minister. That was of course wasted effort on the old man. The priest himself saw it – too late. As for the story about abandoning the decision to cut out diseased cocoa trees, he said that the thing was absolutely impossible. He reminded the Oba that he must have seen how powerful the White Man was. If there was anything that could be done to save the trees, the White Man would have discovered it. But there was nothing, nothing whatsoever. About that he was absolutely certain. 'How very much I myself wish that the gossip was true. How I wish that the God of Harvest would bestow His mercy upon His children and Himself remove this dreadful scourge from our land. I still pray night and day and will continue to pray night and day that God Himself deliver us from this great tribulation at no distant date. But up till today our prayers are still to be answered. I implore you, Your Highness, owner of Ipaja, not to allow men of straw to raise your hopes unnecessarily and to oppose the Administration in whatever measures they think best to take against the cocoa disease. To do that is to kick against the pricks.'

The priest was done. He had warmed to his subject, and by the end his voice rang out with the conviction of gospel truth, as if he were speaking from the pulpit of his own church.

The Oba sighed, apparently convinced. 'I salute you, Pastor, I salute you, welcome,' he said. 'I thank you for all the words that you have said. They are the words of wisdom and truth. Since you have been in our town, as a teacher and as priest, we have never seen anything bad against you. You said something just now, Pastor. About kicking against the pricks. If a man kicks against the pricks, will the pricks not hurt him? Will they not? – answer me —'

Olaiya nodded.

'And do the pricks suffer – do they?'

Again Olaiya nodded. The pricks do not suffer.

'But Reverend, you know we are not educated – my chiefs and I are not educated. You are educated, and you know the ways of the White Man and what he wants. Mr Benjamin Benjamin is educated and he knows the ways of the White Man and the lawyers. Both of you are educated. You read the same books. But you confuse us who are not educated. You tell us different things. Yet you read the same books. Why then do you read different things from the same books? That is why my chiefs and I are confused. We do not know who to follow. We are no longer masters of ourselves. Reverend,

Reverend, Reverend, I want to say something . . . the world is now a spoilt world—'

After his visitor had left the Oba came back to his sleeping-room where he had left his other visitor. He told him who it was and what they had discussed. Chief Olowokere the Obanla heard the Oba in silence. Then he said simply: 'Your Highness, what shall we do about it?'

'What shall we do about it? That is word. Obanla, what shall we do about it?'

Again the Obanla was silent. The two of them were silent. The Oba adjusted the wick of the lamp.

The Obanla was the first to speak. 'You know Reverend does not like Benja-Benja. They do not like each other. . . . Reverend is jealous of the greater education of Benja-Benja. The education of Reverend is out of date. He cannot write a letter that can go beyond Apeno. He can even hardly write as far as the capital. Whereas Benja-Benja can write as far as London. He wrote to the White Man's King.'

'You don't say – Benja-Benja the man!'

'Benja-Benja has great influence with the men who write news in the newspapers. He knows all the people in the big Government offices in the city. . . . See how he won the case against Government – don't you see that he has extraordinary powers and connexions?'

'The boy uses a wonderful juju. Benja-Benja, the man.'

'The juju he uses is from India. It is called a Talisman. It is very powerful. It is through it he spoke to the King of England and told him to instruct the Government here that he should be made Prime Minister and that our cocoa farms should be left undisturbed. The boy is a wizard.'

CHAPTER TWENTY-THREE

On the wide veranda of the Residency at Apeno, Stanfield read for a second time the letter passed on by the Chief Commissioner for the Central Protectorate. He had brought it over from the office in order to discuss it with Henry Gregory, now Acting Senior Provincial Agricultural Officer, whom he was expecting for lunch.

> His Excellency the Governor has received a communication from the Secretary of State for the Colonies reporting the very encouraging news that the research work which has been in progress for some time at the Imperial College of Tropical Agriculture, under the able guidance of Dr E. M. Rodent, has reached a stage where His Majesty's Government can now say with a certain degree of confidence that it will not be long before a cure for the cocoa disease is announced. The letter from the Colonial Office also gives details of successful experiments carried out on model cocoa farms in Brazil. The disease was induced artificially in trees at various stages of growth, and the chemical evolved by the Imperial College of Agriculture in collaboration with a firm of industrial chemists was applied with very encouraging results.
>
> 2. The letter from the Colonial Office does not emphasize the importance which Dr Rodent's discovery will have for the economy of this country and for the prestige of British science and of Britain. His Excellency wishes to enlist the cooperation of all Residents and senior Administrative Officers in publicizing the far-reaching value of Dr Rodent's work and in underlining that it is British scientists who have saved this country's cocoa. It is important to publicize the fact that they have been financed entirely by the British taxpayer. At a time when our model colonial policy is undergoing strong criticism from agitators from

within and without the territory (including some misguided British citizens at home) the impact of this information could be of the greatest political value. If publicity is organized on these lines, the detribalized politicians of the coast should experience greater difficulty in obtaining support for their 'anti-imperialist' campaigns from farmers who will realize that it is British money and British skill which have preserved their wealth.

3. His Excellency will keep Residents, Senior Administrative Officers and Senior Agricultural Officers posted on any new developments reported by the Colonial Office from the Imperial College of Tropical Agriculture. Government House is in close contact with the West Indies.

I have the honour to be,
Sir,
Your obedient servant,

M. St Anthony
Acting Deputy Secretary

With the letter was a brief biography of Dr Rodent:

Edward Melville Rodent (born August 20th, 1901) is the only son of Major Edward and Mrs Amelia Rodent of 146, Leeds Road, Idle, near Bradford. After attending Bradford Grammar School, he went up to Pembroke College, Cambridge, where he gained a blue for cricket and a half blue for athletics, and achieved a First-Class in the first part of his Tripos, but left without completing his degree. He served in his father's old regiment in India, and was wounded on the North-West Frontier. He then picked up the threads of his education at the University of Manchester, where he gained a First-Class Honours degree and followed it with a Ph.D. in an unmapped area of *Virus Diseases of Tropical Plants*. He lectured for a number of years at Manchester University and then at the University of London. He was for four years on the senior staff of the Research Section of Kew Gardens and appointed head of the Plant Diseases Department of the Imperial College of Tropical Agriculture in 1943.

Dr Rodent is married to Rosa Wilhelmina, second daughter of the Rev. and Mrs John Angus of Middlesborough, Yorkshire. They have two sons aged 17 and 12. His chief hobby is amateur dramatics.

Just as Stanfield finished reading the letter, Henry Gregory's car drew up. He came up the veranda steps and sank into one of the deck-chairs. He asked the white-uniformed steward for a brandy-ginger, and sipped it with appreciation.

'Startling news about Rodent's discovery,' said Stanfield as he watched his guest. 'What do you Agriculture chaps think about it?'

'Well, there seems to be some hush-hush about the real details of the thing,' replied Gregory, 'and, as usual, the Colonial Office release doesn't tell one much. It's a pity they didn't attach a history of the research project and less about Rodent. One has of course heard hints for months from the Imperial College chaps.'

'Of course, Henry. I'd forgotten you went to that Conference in Trinidad.'

'Yes, I did – and rather regretted it. I had to cancel my leave arrangements to go mountaineering in the Alps, and take the plane to the West Indies instead. Same old tropical climate made rather worse by being thrown into the company of a bunch of professors from China to Peru. One's research colleagues are always so repulsive in the mass. The whole Conference was an absolute waste of time.'

'Surely you got something out of it, old boy. You must have had a look at Rodent's work.'

'Oh yes. At that time he had already isolated the virus. Fascinating-looking thing under the microscope. A sort of hydra-headed monster – real African juju.'

'Most interesting.'

'And what's more interesting is the complicated apparatus the chaps designed for observing the effects of various chemical compounds on the monster. The chap who took us round explained it. An incomprehensible number of permutations and combinations of organic chemistry, parasitology, tropical agriculture, climatology, calculus, geology and of course African juju – all taken two at a time. Then to the result add plain common sense and start all over again. That was Rodent's recipe.'

'But, seriously,' said Stanfield, 'it's a revolutionary discovery.

One of the best things that has happened in our colonial history in Africa. Bound to have pretty far-reaching results.'

'Of course, of course. It's a fearfully epoch-making discovery that a compound of mercury will kill a virus, isn't it?' Gregory replied ironically. 'We all learnt that in elementary chemistry at school. Still it's a new and sensational invention which we owe to our kinsman Teddy Rodent, O.B.E., Ph.D., etcetera! His laboratory and staff have cost the British taxpayer well nigh one hundred thousand pounds so far, do you know?'

Both men were silent for some time. Then Gregory said: 'I see that chap in Ipaja, the rascal that has christened himself after one of the tribes of Israel—'

'Benjamin Benjamin.'

'Yes, Benjamin Benjamin; a most ingenious name, has rather a romantic flavour to it too. Well, I see he's already disputing credit for the discovery with Rodent. A weird exhibition – an English scientist and a half-baked African rabble-rouser disputing over a thing like that. One made his discovery through scientific methods, the other from African juju, alias Black science. I suppose they are both right. After all, they have a common ancestor in Noah; he deserves the credit for the discovery.'

At this point Jim Stanfield rose and led the way to the dining-room.

Jim Stanfield liked Gregory, and had always maintained that he had a bright future in the Colonial Agricultural Service. That young Henry should now be acting Senior Provincial Agricultural Officer was proof enough that Stanfield's confidence had not been misplaced. But certain aspects of Gregory's character worried him: often he found him jarringly flippant.

Stanfield had been long enough in the Service to feel that a certain amount of traditional British humour may leaven the work of an administrator, and make the going less tedious. Good for the digestion. Good for the blood pressure. But Gregory seemed to carry this attitude to extremes.

Take Gregory's attitude to the new discovery, for instance. Carefree, irresponsible. In Stanfield's view, Gregory should be considering how the discovery would affect his Department's policy and activities.

One thing had given Stanfield misgivings even before Gregory's arrival. He was dubious about the wisdom of sending a copy of the Governor's letter to all Residents, Senior Administrative Officers and Senior Agricultural Officers. Stanfield felt that while it was all very right and proper to rejoice at the achievement of British science, a circular letter from the Secretariat was hardly the most tactful means of doing so. Such a letter in the hands of an old Coaster like himself would probably achieve the desired effect; it was probably most ill-advised to put a document of this kind in the hands of the younger men. Gregory's attitude was a case in point.

True the letter was marked 'Confidential'. But Jim Stanfield had regretfully come to realize that the Gregorys who found themselves in senior positions relatively young were, in the main, unable to keep their mouths shut (and the spreading atmosphere of nationalism meant more Gregorys in senior positions). Stanfield recalled with a qualm the startling disclosures at the Ipaja Inquiry about the 'mislaid' confidential file in the Secretariat.

At a time when Africans had started to come into the Administrative Service it was surely unwise to circulate such a letter. It was Government policy to appoint more and more Africans to senior posts and Africans, even of the calibre of Akpan, would resent the self-congratulatory tone of the letter. Stanfield still genuinely believed in Akpan; he had written a laudatory confidential report on him only the previous month. 'Integrity beyond reproach. . . . Ability outstanding. . . . In all respects a fine young man who is a credit to his race, and indeed to any race.' He knew that Akpan had been little affected by the irresponsible nationalism around him. But he was an African and a patriot.

'Massa no want soup?'

Jim Stanfield was startled from his day-dreaming by the steward. 'Soup? Of course I want soup, Yisa.' He looked at his companion, already half-way through the main course.

Stanfield sighed.

The following day he sent a letter to Udo Akpan.

I have received a confidential letter from the Commissioner for the Central Protectorate in which he gives information about the latest development in the research work that has been going on in the study of the cocoa disease virus at the Imperial College of Tropical Agriculture, and the result of control experiments that have been carried out on the cocoa plantations in the adjoining territory in South America.

2. This letter gives no directives as to what the Administration should do in the District at this stage. I am still in consultation with the office of the Commissioner on this subject. I am told by the Senior Research Officer (Cocoa) that a lot of work remains to be done on the subject and that the Department of Agriculture cannot at this stage say anything with any degree of certainty. We can, however, assume that a cure for the cocoa disease which will not involve the cutting down of trees is now in sight. There must therefore be a review of the standing policy of wholesale eradication of plantations of diseased trees.

3. Until the position is clearer please take no further action on the decision to resume cutting-out operations on farms in the Ipaja–Apeno District, which you said you have planned to start in the near future. This, incidentally, is fortunate, as I had a telephone call from the Deputy Commissioner of Police last night that the entire C Division of the Force (from which the Cocoa Disease Squad were to come) have now been moved to the border to quell some terrorist activities that are causing grave anxiety to the Government.

4. I am now finalizing my arrangements for my next tour. If all goes well, I should leave here on the 5th and return on the 17th. I just must tear myself away from the files here and do the tour, as I have already postponed it three times. When I come you must come round to discuss the Sports Club – you must tell me about that 65 I hear you knocked up for the Protectorate last week, to revive the waning glory of Protectorate Cricketing.

Yours sincerely,
James Stanfield
Acting Resident

Jim Stanfield was right in his suspicion that the office of the Chief Commissioner might not have exercised much discretion in the distribution of the circular letter from the Governor's Office. Udo Akpan had received a copy of it two days before the arrival of Stanfield's letter.

CHAPTER TWENTY-FOUR

Udo Akpan's letter of resignation stunned Jim Stanfield.

He read it a second time. It was addressed in stiff official language to the Chief Secretary to the Government, 'through the Chief Commissioner for the Protectorate, through the Senior Administrative Officer, through the Acting Resident'.

After long and anxious consideration I have decided to resign my appointment as Administrative Officer Grade I in the Civil Service, with effect from one month of the date of this letter.

I am not required under the Civil Service Code to give reasons for my resignation. I will, however, state here that it has been apparent to me for some time as an Administrative Officer both in my former station and here in the Ipaja–Apeno District that the meagre resources at the disposal of Government are woefully inadequate for tackling the immense problem of African administration. My honest efforts as a cog in the huge wheel of Government have been completely stultified by the fact that I have access only to the minutest fraction of the policy of Government, thanks to the men who make this policy both in this country and in Whitehall. The little of this policy that came out through a slit in the great policy machine two days ago has convinced me that as an African I can no longer identify myself with the execution of this policy.

It is my conviction that I can be of greater service to my race and my God in an entirely different capacity where my humble efforts will not be fettered by General Orders, Financial Instructions, and other aspects of Civil Service bureaucracy which together have rendered the Administration helpless, made our adopted system of justice an object of ridicule and will before long bring a complete disintegration of law and order in the country.

Jim Stanfield was still holding the letter in his hand and was pacing up and down the veranda, when Henry Gregory came in.

He sank into a chair, thoroughly exhausted. 'Uh. . . . Temperature 89°. Humidity 90%. Virus concentration in the air, billions to the cubic millimetre. God's own country that we are stealing from the Black Man. . . . But what is the matter, old man?'

'Udo Akpan has sent in a letter of resignation. Here.'

'Oh no,' Henry Gregory said in surprise. He reached out for the letter. 'The old boy won't let us down like that. Why, we were training him to be the first Governor of this all-black dominion.'

There was silence for a moment. Gregory read through the letter while Stanfield smoked nervously.

'The fellow's mad,' Gregory concluded, handing the letter back to his companion.

'I just cannot understand it. Doesn't make sense.' Stanfield was speaking more to himself than to Gregory.

'Uh, little that these chaps do does make sense, Jim.'

'Henry, I wish you wouldn't talk like that.'

Gregory knew that Stanfield was usually infinitely tolerant of his attitude. This mild rebuke was the height of disapproval.

'Oh, I know how you feel about it, old man. Magnificent fellow, and all that. But what's the sense in this? Fellow throws up wonderful job for no reasons at all.'

'Udo Akpan has his reasons.'

'Oh, read that letter again, man. Read it again. Long strings of words that really don't convey any meaning. The fellow just hasn't got a meaning for his action anyway.'

'Just why do you say that, Henry?'

'Right. Half the words he'd used were lifted bodily from the abdication statement of old Edward. For your Akpan's "resign my appointment" substitute "renounce the throne". And that is how your Udo Akpan started – as if he was renouncing a throne.'

'Throwing up a top civil service job is a very serious matter.'

'Of course it is. Edward Rex at least gave logical reasons why he was renouncing his throne. And all the world saw it. But read through that letter again. One long piece of generalization. Very vague, from beginning to end.'

The two men were again silent for a moment. Stanfield lit his fourth cigarette. Gregory broke the silence. 'Well, what are you going to do about it?'

'Resignation not accepted,' Stanfield said.

'I'm not sure that the Resident has the power to accept or reject resignations of officers of the seniority of Akpan. You may wish to have a refresher course in the Civil Service bible on the subject.'

'If it is the last thing I do, Gregory,' Jim Stanfield said thoughtfully, slowly, 'I must make sure that Udo Akpan remains in the Civil Service of this country.'

Udo Akpan recognized Jim Stanfield's car as it pulled up in his drive. He got up from the writing-desk and, slipping his dressing-gown over his pyjamas, went to open the door.

'Sorry to bother you at this time of the day, Udo. Thought I'd have a chat with you straight away. I'm sorry to disturb your rest. May I sit down?'

'Do sit down, sir. Quite a surprise.'

It might surprise Akpan that the Acting Resident had come to see him in his own house at three o'clock – that he had not sent for him to come to him at the Residency. But it was no surprise to him that Jim Stanfield had decided to discuss with him his letter of resignation.

Jim Stanfield was aware of this too.

'The chap at your telephone exchange must be dead or something. I tried to ring three times. Decided it was easier to drive down than hanging on on the telephone. You are well, Udo?'

'Very well, thank you, sir. Have a cigarette.'

'Thank you.'

They were both silent. Jim Stanfield lit his cigarette from the match Udo struck and held out to him. He looked round the room.

Stanfield broke the silence. 'Udo, I've come to give you back this,' he said, handing to him an unsealed, unaddressed foolscap envelope. 'I'm sure you've slept on it, and decided to withdraw the letter.'

Udo extracted the three sheets from the envelope. He noticed that the Resident had not made any comments on them, had not even initialled them. They were not even date-stamped at the Resident's Office.

'I certainly have slept on it. But I've decided not to withdraw it.'

Again there was a short silence. Then Stanfield said, 'Udo, why do you want to resign?'

'I feel I can no longer be Administrative Officer in the circumstances prevailing in the Service.'

'Why, what's wrong with the Service?'

'Everything.'

Jim Stanfield knew he had asked a silly question: he knew very well there were many things wrong with the Service. But of course Udo was just being childish and vague, when he said everything was wrong with the Service. However, he was not going to demonstrate the young man's stupidity, which might well stiffen his resistance.

'Look here, Udo, you really don't mean that it is all things that are wrong with the Service. Which things are the immediate cause of your wanting to resign?'

'The letter you wrote concerning the latest development in the cocoa disease research, and the decision to change our policy about the cutting out of diseased trees.'

The Englishman looked puzzled. 'But why should that make you leave the Service, Udo? We are all happy for you and your countrymen about the discovery. Surely you see the tremendous effect it is going to have on the economy of the country. And, which is equally important, on the politics here as far as the Administration is concerned. You see the point, surely, Udo?'

'Very well, sir, I see it quite clearly.'

'Well?'

'But someone else saw the point too. He was in possession of official information addressed only to Senior Administrative Officers and marked "Confidential". He was in possession of it long before me.'

'Oh, that. You know what these newspaper boys are. The same all over the world the way they get hold of the most secret information, and twist it in blazing headlines to embarrass the Government.'

'I think it is bad enough for official information that is secret to get into the newspapers. But what has happened here is worse. Benjamin Benjamin was in possession of the information before it was published in *National Affairs*. He had twisted the facts to suit his own purpose. He'd told the people of Ipaja that he was responsible for the decision of Government to abandon the cutting down of cocoa trees. And they believed him. And, what's worse, I advised them that Benjamin Benjamin was lying and that Government had taken no such decision and would not take such decision. That was before I had your letter. I dare not show my face at Ipaja now. They'd stone me.'

'I see your difficulty. I'm sorry, Udo.'

Again both men were silent for some time. Again it was Stanfield who spoke first. 'But Udo, we really do not know whose fault it was that Benjamin Benjamin had advance information about the cocoa disease discovery. Same source as the newspaper's, no doubt. But that wasn't your fault. We treat such things with the contempt they deserve. And carry on with our work. That's what we do.' He crushed the stump of his cigarette in the ashtray: he took out his cigarette case and offered one to Udo.

'When I took over this District you emphasized to me the importance of persuading the people to agree to total eradication of diseased trees. All my efforts have been geared to the preaching of this gospel. No known cure for the disease, we all preached. From their own intuition and hatred of self-inflicted destruction the farmers protested, and made our work difficult. We told them they were wrong, and that they were fools. . . .

'Now we are to go back to them and say we were wrong. A wonderful discovery has now been made, a wonderful cure found for the cocoa disease. We who until a week ago were insisting on their cutting out all diseased trees will this week take back all the things we'd been saying.'

'But, Udo, this is something to do with the march of science. Nothing to do with us. And as it happens in this case, the people will welcome the development.'

'They will welcome the development all right. But they will not welcome me, or anything I may say in future. That's the point, sir.'

'Oh dear, oh dear.'

'It is most amazing, when our Government, through the Colonial Office, commissioned Dr Rodent to do research work into the cocoa disease virus, that it did not occur to us that there was the possibility, perhaps the probability that Rodent might discover the virus and the cure for the disease. If Government knew that, how could it preach the gospel of wholesale eradication of diseased trees, to the extent that it has created a most serious problem for those of us who are the unfortunate ones to face the farmers? It is astonishing that it did not occur to anyone that the obvious thing to do was to wait a while till the result of Rodent's work was known. At least till there was some indication one way or the other.

'And of course the detractors of Government did not fail to take advantage of Government's blunder. Benjamin Benjamin told the people that the cutting-out campaign was a deliberate act of wickedness on the part of Government to oppress the farmers. And of course they believed him. I don't blame them. I myself would believe that wickedness would be the only explanation for such a thing. Or insanity. And if I were in

Benjamin Benjamin's position seeking political power, I would do exactly what he has done. Take advantage of the muddled-thinking and short-sighted policy of Government. I'm sorry, but—'

The Englishman saw that the young man was speaking with a great deal of feeling. 'I am sorry for you, Udo. Believe me, I'm very sorry.'

'This man Benjamin Benjamin has been allowed to take advantage of the great weaknesses in our Administration to fool the people and the Administration all the time. I spent nearly four weeks of my valuable time inquiring into his fund-raising activities at Ipaja. I listened to the evidence of his victims and of his accomplices during the day. I went back to do my normal office work at night. The fellow showed the greatest disrespect to me by refusing to come to the Inquiry. The legal people took months to decide that there was a case for criminal proceedings against him and his associates. It again took months before the case got into the courts. And the result? Benjamin Benjamin had known he would be discharged and acquitted right from the beginning of the case. He had seen to that through the wonderful efficiency and integrity of the prosecution that charged him under the wrong section of the law.'

'Oh no, Udo. I know how you feel about this matter. I know how disappointed you must feel after the case. But you are not suggesting that the prosecution – the Crown – deliberately charged the fellow under the wrong section of the law!'

'And one more thing, sir. While in your letter you only referred to His Excellency's letter about Rodent's discovery, the Secretariat actually sent me a copy of His Excellency's letter.' Udo went on, having noted the effect of his revelation on his companion's face. 'His Excellency's letter in my opinion was more a glorification of the achievement of British Science than joy at the discovery of something that will bring prosperity to the African farmer. I am of the opinion that if that letter is any indication to go by, there is no self-respecting African who would want to identify himself with the present set-up. There is just no future for the African in the present set-up of the administration of his own country. And I have made up my mind to get out before I am set in the rut, before I am too old in the service to make a new start outside it.'

'Oh dear, Udo. I know how you feel. Still—'

The telephone rang.

'District Officer,' Udo said into the receiver.

'Is that the house of the D.O.?' asked the voice at the other end.

'Yes. This is the District Officer.'

'May I speak to D.O.?' said the voice.

'For the third time, this is the District Officer. Who's speaking, and what do you want?'

'I want D.O.'

Udo was exasperated.

'Listen, I am D.O. Now what do you want?'

'Oh. Good afternoon, sir. This is A.S.P. from Police Station, Ipaja. There are serious riots here. Many houses—'

'Good Lord, riots in Ipaja!'

'Yes, sir. Serious riots, sir. Many houses have been destroyed, many people —'

'What? What? Can you hear me?'

Silence. The telephone connexion had been broken. 'Operator, Operator, Operator—'

No answer.

'Operator, Operator, Operator—'

Nothing. Absolutely nothing.

'Ring the Postmaster's house,' Jim Stanfield suggested.

'Operator, Operator, Operator—'

'Number, please?' said a voice charged with sleep.

'I want Ipaja Police Station. Immediately.'

'Number, please!'

'Ipaja Police Station. Urgent.'

'Is that D.O.? Good afternoon, sir. Wait a moment, sir. . . .

Everybody, clear the line,' Udo heard the telephone operator order on the trunk line. 'D.O. wants to speak to Ipaja. . . . Ipaja, Ipaja, Ipaja. . . . Oh, the operator at Ipaja must be sleeping. If D.O. should know that and report to Controller now, then they will accuse me of being responsible for this operator losing his job. What am I to do now, eh? . . . Ipaja, Ipaja, Ipaja. . . . Is that D.O.?'

'Yes, D.O. here. Have you got Ipaja?'

'No, sir. I'm sorry, sir. Ipaja line is out of order.'

CHAPTER TWENTY-FIVE

It is now difficult to tell exactly when and how that afternoon the riots first started – it is almost impossible to determine the borderline between a rowdy meeting in which a few people get hurt, and riots in which houses are destroyed and men are seriously wounded and killed.

Since the discharge and acquittal of Benjamin Benjamin and his associates from the charges of stealing and conspiracy there had been a series of disorderly meetings in Ipaja, most of them the work of Benjamin Benjamin himself. But a number of them were organized and addressed by lieutenants and comrades whenever Benjamin Benjamin was away from Ipaja or was otherwise engaged.

The people of Ipaja had come to associate these meetings with hooliganism, and except for the lorry boys and schoolboy truants who had nobody to keep check on their movements, most self-respecting people now kept away from them for fear of their lives. But the people still believed in Benjamin Benjamin: they just didn't want to get hurt. But whatever the attendance at the meetings lacked in quality, it gained in quantity.

What appeared to be no more than another routine meeting in the campaign now known as 'One man, One matchet' was taking place at the lorry park that afternoon. The attendance was not larger than previous meetings, indeed perhaps a little less. But the organizers would never have admitted that their leader's influence was on the wane.

Benjamin Benjamin spoke. He went over the familiar grounds of the wickedness of the foreign imperialists and the inefficiency and dishonesty of their hirelings, the African District Officer and the Church.

He said he hated to attack a whole organization as a few individual members were no doubt good, conscientious and God-fearing; followers of the simple Jesus of Nazareth. But as long as these few honest men of God continued to harbour in their midst bigots and imperialist agents like Josiah Olaiya the good ones must be prepared to suffer the consequences of their unwisdom – they must all be lumped together for condemnation in the wrath to come. He spoke of how it was just a matter of days and perhaps hours before the Government of the country would be forced to announce to them at Ipaja that Government had failed and that he, Benjamin Benjamin, had won the battle.

He concluded with the campaign slogan, 'One man, One matchet'. No one could tell, however, who took up the chant, 'One man, One matchet'.

'One man, One matchet.' A few more repeated the slogan.

'One woman, One stick,' the same voice led again.

'One woman, One stick,' the crowd cried after him, louder and louder.

'One child, One stone.'

'One child, One stone,' the crowd shouted in dangerous frenzy.

Then someone chanted the first line of one of the inter-tribal war songs – forgotten now except when a great man of inter-tribal war fame died and one of the very few remaining bards of the land sang at his funeral. The words of the song maddened and excited the crowd even more.

Immediately surrounding the lorry park were rows of shops. One of them belonged to a Syrian, and stocked a wide range of articles, from cycles and sewing-machines to safety matches and lamps. In a body the crowd made for this shop. They assaulted and scared away the protesting shopowner and his assistants and helped themselves to anything that presented itself.

First to go were the matchets which were stocked in fairly good quantities in anticipation of the need of the Ipaja farmers. They were now commandeered by the Ipaja patriots in obedience to the call of *One man, One matchet!* Four shot-guns went – the usual preliminary of obtaining the prescribed permit from the District Officer forgotten in the excitement. Then followed articles like axes and shovels and rakes and basins and buckets. What did it matter what they were designed for?

While the main body of looters moved to the remaining shops a few stayed behind to help themselves to free drinks – brandy, gin, whisky. Unused to such extravagance, they were soon affected by the strong spirits. The rest went in search of more loot in the direction of the market square.

Not far from the square they met a truck that carried its motto on big plates both front and back: *No Accident.* The rioters refused to give way to *No Accident.* The driver was unused to crowds of people milling about in the middle of the road and refusing to give way. Women usually scurried to safety at the sight of him: his driving was notorious. He was too late in reacting to the situation. He pressed his hand on the horn; no one paid any attention. He shut his eyes tightly as he put his right foot hard down on the brake pedal. He pressed it hard. Too hard. Then for a long time he remembered nothing.

When he opened his eyes again he saw that his beloved *No Accident* was lying on its back on the road verge. Its four wheels were in the air. He saw littered all over the place – carriageway, verge and drain – the cartons of cigarettes which was the principal cargo he was carrying from the capital to Apeno via Ipaja. And he saw a number of the rioters making away with them. He attempted to get up to stop the looting. But he fell back as he felt the pain in his left ankle.

'Thieves!' he yelled in anguish. He burst into tears.

The main stream of rioters pressed on carrying matchets and sticks, singing war chants and obscene songs. They brandished the weapons and gestured to people who watched from the safety of their verandas and behind their windows, calling to them to come and join them in the riots.

The mob stopped in front of the two-storey building of Chief Olowokere, the Obanla of Ipaja. It was one of the first houses to be built in sandcrete blocks set in cement mortar. No professional architects prepared the plans. No professional surveyors prepared any bills of quantities. No professional builders were engaged in the construction of the house that contained the two parlours and twelve rooms in which Olowo and his eight wives and twenty-three children and relatives lived. But in spite of all this 'Olowo Mansion', finished in bright colours, was the most famous house in Ipaja and was one of the important sights to which visitors to Ipaja were taken.

The family of Chief Olowo were surprised when someone in the front line of the mob sang a hostile song. Olowo was known to be a supporter of Benjamin Benjamin, both before he became a chief and after. He was a very popular citizen and chief, and it was known that but for his status he might have taken part in the demonstrations.

The Olowo household did not wait long to discuss the impending attack. Some started to lock the doors and barricade themselves in the rooms. A number of young men and women escaped through the back into the compounds of near-by houses.

The attackers went to work. They smashed the windows. They broke down a door at the rear on the ground floor. They smashed up chairs and tables. They smashed up two cupboards full of crockery – dishes and plates and cups and tumblers, most of which were only used for decoration. They were kept in the glass cupboards to be admired, to be envied by the less fortunate callers.

In one of the rooms on the ground floor and known to be forbidden to other inmates of the house the rioters brought out what was said to be Olowo's juju and main source of financial strength. It was the skull of what might have been a dog. It was hung over the door, draped with a crimson-red leather belt strung with cowrie shells. It was brought down with a matchet stroke, and the dry skull and the cowries scattered in all directions. Some of the rioters were not beyond recognizing the danger of taking any liberties with juju, consequences of which could be disastrous. They ran away from the room into the backyard lest the juju include them together with the condemned. Others who were not aware of their peril or who merely dared the consequences sat down on the dusty, cobweb-ridden bed in the room.

Many more people crowded together on the single, narrow timber staircase than it could carry. Regardless of their danger a number of these began to matchet the joists and floor boards of the first landing. The rickety structure gave way under the combination of assault and the weight of the assailants.

The account that reached the little village of Abebe said that their Liege Lord the Oba Apaja of Ipaja had declared war on their old enemy the Oba of Apeno. And led by five of their hunters the men of Abebe marched in a procession into Ipaja, singing war songs, and firing their dane guns. At the entrance to the town they fired a particularly heavy salvo. In one single stroke one of them, a huge, sulky-looking rustic, severed the head from a dog that barked as if in warning to the towns-people. Two of the hunters dabbled their hands in the blood while the headless trunk of the animal still involuntarily quivered.

The procession of village men on the war-path proceeded up the main road towards the town centre, firing their guns, singing their war songs against the Apenos. One more dog, two goats and several ducks were slaughtered as the gang passed the animals on their way. More men joined in the procession as it approached the town centre. But, unlike other processions that were a regular feature of the town, there were no women and children. The children were forbidden by their mothers to leave the safety of the verandas of the houses where the women themselves watched what was happening, while they held their breasts and panted in fear of the outcome of it all.

Outside the compound of an old chief of inter-tribal war fame the procession stopped. The old chief came out. He did not come right out to the road, but stayed in his outer veranda, draped in a loin-cloth, and leaning heavily on his walking-stick and chewing some alligator pepper. He spat out the stuff and raised a well-known war song usually sung to commemorate a victory in the inter-tribal wars. Those in the crowd that knew the song joined in. And a few joined in the strange dance, a combination of acrobatics and dancing. One minute the dancers danced singly, completely oblivious of the presence of the other dancers. Next minute, they engaged each other in what looked like a real life-or-death combat. More and more men began to join in the war-dance, after they had watched for some time and convinced themselves that they had mastered the technique. Then the old chief called for silence and he proceeded to bless the army of the Ipajas and to curse the people of Apeno.

The Abebe men were still flushed with the inspiration they had received from the old warrior chief when they came to the post-office building. The post-master was an Apeno and therefore a marked man. He and his staff had locked up hastily and fled at the first sign of trouble.

The rioters climbed on to the wide veranda, and soon the floor was littered with broken glass from the window panes.

One of the men regarded for a moment the wire coming out from under the eaves of the building. His eye followed it to the top of the pole on the post-office side of the road. He saw the wire wrapped round some small white object on the top of the pole, slung across the road and connected to a similar object on another pole on the other side of that road. He looked farther down the road and saw a series of similar poles and the same wire slung from pole to pole. He had always seen them, hundreds of them along the road from Ipaja, past his dear Abebe, and on to Apeno. He had never bothered to know the mystery of the wire slung from pole to pole. Today was as good as any other for exploring the mystery. With one stroke he severed the wire a few inches from the fascia board of the roof of the post office.

At that moment the conversation between Udo Akpan at Apeno and the police sergeant at Ipaja ceased.

The Rev. Josiah Olaiya was sure that, crazed though the rioters might be, they would never attack the House of the Lord in the shape of the church of St John's. Nor would any of them dare lay his hand on the Lord's anointed. However mad a dog might be, would it not recognize (and so run away from) a fire? Would it not?

Olaiya was quite right. For when the main body of rioters reached the church building they merely went past, singing, shouting, but giving no indication that they were going to attack the building. Again when they were passing the front of the parsonage the rioters disregarded the presence of the vicar with his wife and three of his children watching them from a window.

Not long after the rioters had left the veranda and sitting-room of the parsonage filled with men and women, neighbours of the clergyman and his family, three of them staunch members of his flock, arguing fiercely about the causes and the consequences of the riots.

One of the men interpreted the whole thing in terms of the prophecy relating to the Last Day. Had it not been said in the Holy Scriptures, he reminded his audience, that on the Last Day there would be wars and rumours of war? that there would be heresies and schisms? Had it not been said that son would turn against father and brother turn against brother? He turned his freckled, wizened face to the priest to confirm his interpretation of the events of the day. But he saved Olaiya the embarrassment of disagreeing, as he did not wait for an answer.

'Take the attack on the house of Chief Olowokere, the Obanla, for instance. I was there, three doors away. And I saw it all with my own eyes. Do you know the attack was led by Olowo's own brother – Joel. I saw it all myself,' he repeated, chewing tobacco.

'His own brother,' Olaiya muttered. 'I don't think I remember him much. He doesn't come to church.'

'But,' one of the men cried out. 'What can anyone do to the Ifa Oracle without its betraying in its behaviour its palm kernel ancestry? Will a bastard not always behave like a bastard? Who here does not know that the mother of Joel was one month pregnant for an Apeno man before she ran back from Apeno and made her husband lie with her? That was why she died the day she gave birth to the bastard. And that is why till today the curse of the bastard son has been a plague in the household.'

But the man of the Armaggedon prophecy gave other reasons for his interpretation. In all the long history of Ipaja, had they ever heard of a black District Officer? Also were they not witnessing a rising against the government of the White Man? Were they not seeing fellow citizens being destroyed? Were they not seeing fellow citizens being wounded? What else did they want as proof?

One of the women sobbed in motherly anxiety over the safety of her son who worked in a government office in the capital. 'I told him to take a teaching job here,' she complained. 'But he said he wanted to go and work in the big city. And now the world has come to an end. And he is not here with me. . . .'

When he had got rid of the last of his overwrought guests Olaiya could not settle down again to the church building accounts. The excitement and fear in the air disturbed him and he could not concentrate.

When his wife came in a short while later she found him dressing to go out. She looked at him critically, lovingly. A blue poplin shirt under a suit of tussore, brown tennis shoes, with heels. As he was trying to adjust his newly-starched dog-collar his wife mentioned that no one ought to be out on a day like that. But he assured her that he would come to no harm, and she readily accepted his assurance. She had learnt to accept his better judgement and knowledge in all things – except money – in their nineteen years of married life. And she knew that there was really nothing to fear. Who would think of harming Pastor, as he was affectionately called?

So the vicar took his walking-stick and his black hat, bade his wife good-bye, and walked out into the street. From that moment the Rev. Josiah Olaiya of St John's, Ipaja, became a missing person.

CHAPTER TWENTY-SIX

When it had become quite dark the vicar's wife smothered the first signs of anxiety over her husband's safety. She persuaded herself that he was really not at all late in coming home yet. He often went to call on church members at such late hours to settle quarrels between husband and wife; to chide a child for his laziness and bad behaviour; to read comforting passages from the Bible to a bedridden old lady, stubbornly clinging to her painful life.

To comfort herself the vicar's wife repeated to herself Psalm 91.

He that dwelleth in the secret place of the most High shall abide under the shadow of the Almighty . . .

Surely He shall deliver thee from the snare of the fowler, and from the noisome pestilence . . .

Thou shalt not be afraid for the terror by night, nor for the arrow that flieth by day.

Nor for the pestilence that walketh in darkness; nor for the destruction that wasteth at noonday.

A thousand shall fall at thy side, and ten thousand at the right hand; but it shall not come nigh thee.

Only with thine eyes shalt thou behold and see the reward of the wicked.

Because thou has made the Lord which is my refuge, even the most High thy habitation.

There shall no evil befall thee, neither shall any plague come nigh thy dwelling.

For He shall give his angels charge over thee, to keep thee in all thy ways.

They shall bear thee up in their hands, lest thou dash thy foot against a stone.

Thou shalt tread upon the lion and adder; the young lion and the dragon shalt thou trample under thy feet . . .

He shall call upon me, and I will answer him: I will be with him in trouble; I will deliver him, and honour him.

With long life will I satisfy him, and shew him my salvation.

But even this did not allay her fears. She began to doubt the efficacy of her prayers, even though Benjamin Benjamin and the rioters were certainly a danger against which the true Christian was insured according to Psalm 91. Distraught, she rushed to the house of the nearest church member and sobbed out her anxiety about her husband's safety.

The vicar? Of course they had all seen the vicar pass in front of their house. More than that, he had hailed them. Of course nothing could happen to him. Nothing whatsoever.

Had the church member in the next house of call seen the vicar? Oh yes, the vicar had certainly passed that way. True he didn't see him himself, but two of his wives saw him and delivered the vicar's message that he be remembered to their husband.

They all trooped out, the men in the first house and in the second and in the other houses where the vicar was likely to have called. They all followed his wife, some consoling her and giving her assurances that her husband was safe and sound, sure to be at the next house, and some inquiring at the next house.

The vicar? Of course he called in that house. He spent a fairly long time too. But he had left quite a while before. Why, he went in the direction of St John's, and should have been back there long before then.

The search for the missing parson continued till the early hours of the morning. They carried their search to all conceivable places – beyond the houses of church members to a few belonging to Moslems and Shango worshippers with whom the Christian parson would not normally be associated. They carried it to the Palace and to the house of Benjamin Benjamin. And before they called it off, long after midnight, they had searched as far as the Moslem cemetery at the Apeno Gate.

At cockcrow the story of the disappearance of Josiah Olaiya had spread beyond the confines of Ipaja into the whole district.

And it reached the ears of Udo Akpan, District Officer.

Udo Akpan felt in some way responsible for Olaiya's safety, and a greater force than his duty compelled him to trace the man. He remembered the afternoon the vicar had called to ask him about the gossip that Government was going to abandon its stand on the campaign for cutting out cocoa trees. He remembered how he had convinced him that the gossip was unfounded and that it was another act of deliberate mischief by Benjamin Benjamin. He knew how completely the older man had trusted him, and how he had become a faithful exponent of his views, how he had risked unpopularity and even bodily harm to take the stand he had taken. But now he himself had discovered that he had suddenly become a losing horse, and Josiah Olaiya was paying dearly for having backed him. Udo had let him down.

Again he recalled his long interview with Stanfield and how frank he had been. He had not anticipated the riots at all, but they only served to confirm his conviction that the Administration was now completely inadequate for maintaining law and order. A minister of religion had been kidnapped, perhaps murdered, for no other cause than persuading those who had put their trust in him to believe that the Administration knew what was best and would do what was best for the people.

And what about his resignation? Udo Akpan had sent in his letter of resignation before the riots and before the disappearance of Josiah Olaiya, but he felt morally bound to clear up the mess in Ipaja first. He must withdraw his resignation for the moment.

To clear up the mess, Udo Akpan arranged for three divisions of police to be drafted to Ipaja before midday on the day after the riots.

Central Government policemen, Local Authority policemen, white police officers, black police officers. Policemen in neat, tailored tunic shirts and shorts, policemen in baggy shorts, policemen in uniform, policemen in plain clothes. They were there – all shades of them. The little police station at Ipaja swarmed with them.

For week after week they roamed the streets and alleys of Ipaja and of Abebe, asking questions, taking statements. They went from house to house, from village to village. Police vans ran from Ipaja to Apeno, from Apeno to Ipaja.

In the riots six men had been killed and seventeen injured, four of them seriously. Of the nine houses damaged, Chief Olowokere the Obanla's was the one property of substantial value. On a brief visit to his Apeno headquarters from Ipaja Akpan had requested the chief clerk to let him see the most important mail that had come in since he moved to Ipaja, and had been given, as the most important, a letter from an Apeno lawyer who claimed to be the solicitor of Chief Olowokere the Obanla. In the letter were listed several items of damage to his client's modern building at Ipaja and a claim from the Administration for the modest sum of £17,500. This did little to improve Akpan's temper.

The Ipaja riots investigations became complicated by the fact that the Oro Masquerade had also taken place on the night of the riots. Udo Akpan refused to believe that the Oro Dance was not part of the riots, but subsequent evidence showed that the Oro Cult had been performing their annual festival for a week before the riots and that the nocturnal dance of the chief masquerade was merely the closing event of the festival. He was confused as to whether Josiah Olaiya's disappearance had been due to the rioters or to the Oro worshippers. If the first he was probably still held a prisoner under torture in the house of some rascal. If the latter – Udo Akpan shuddered to think what might have happened to him. Udo did not belong to those parts. But he knew what happened to a non-initiate who came out to see the secret, sacred doings of the Oro on the final night of the festival.

Benjamin Benjamin was suspect Number One in the riots. Udo Akpan had no doubt in his mind that he was at the bottom of the whole affair, but he knew in spite of his hatred for the man that he must be very cautious in the way he handled him. He realized that the Administration's life in the District was now suspended by a very thin thread. It could not afford another abortive attempt at catching the trouble-maker of Ipaja.

So instead, Udo Akpan cast his net away from the direction of Benjamin Benjamin. In three days it caught thirteen men – nine from Ipaja, all lieutenants and associates of Benjamin Benjamin, and four from the village of Abebe.

They were sent to the jail house in Apeno. Here Udo Akpan did not care to be cautious about the technical objection to keeping in the prison yard men who had not been formally charged for any offence, and were only in custody pending the outcome of police investigation.

Benjamin Benjamin had discovered that the Administration was avoiding a direct clash with him now and he began to flirt with arrest. He also knew how much he stood to gain from the publicity of being arrested 'in the fight against persecution'. So he made himself a nuisance. One afternoon an outraged police sergeant from the capital charged him for obstructing the police, for behaviour likely to cause a breach of the peace, and for three other offences duly recorded importantly in his pocket book. Benjamin Benjamin cooperated most wonderfully with the police. He was a most willing passenger in the Austin Black Maria that conveyed him from Ipaja to Apeno.

And so, while the search for the missing parson continued at Ipaja, the self-styled First Citizen and Gentleman of Ipaja was appearing before the Magistrate at Apeno, charged with obstructing the police. The less famous citizens of Ipaja led by Chief Olowokere's brother and enemy, were appearing before the same functionary on a charge which made up in gravity for the want in their own importance, the charge of taking part in the riots, causing damages to property, causing bodily harm to persons named and enumerated in the charge sheet, and causing directly or indirectly the death of seven fellow citizens of Ipaja again named and enumerated in the charge sheet.

The case of obstructing the police was withdrawn. When the Police Prosecutor begged permission of the magistrate to withdraw the case, the magistrate remarked that the police should make up their minds before bringing charges. Benjamin Benjamin laughed and the magistrate turned on him sharply.

'I do not know and I do not care to know the reasons why the charge of obstructing the police has been withdrawn. And while you may have cause for joy, I must warn you that this is a court of law and not a village lorry park where you address your followers on a soap box. I shall not hesitate to have you charged for contempt of court here and now.'

'Your Worship, I rise to apologize on behalf of my client,' his counsel said, holding the lapels of his jacket. 'I assure Your Worship that my client means no disrespect to this honourable court, and less so to Your Worship. The incident is most unfortunate, and is regretted.'

The accused persons in the riots case pleaded not guilty. The case was adjourned. Benjamin Benjamin's request to bail them was treated with contempt. The men were once more locked up in custody in the prison yard.

Like the proverbial bad penny, Benjamin Benjamin turned up again at the Ipaja lorry park. And while there, telling to a crowd of his supporters the story of his gallant bid to bail the 'nationalists, the brave sons of Ipaja, and victims of oppression', he was shot dead by Chief Olowokere, the Obanla of Ipaja.

CHAPTER TWENTY-SEVEN

It was clear that the Chief needed no second shot for Benjamin Benjamin. He turned the gun upon himself and fired into his own neck. He cried out as he fell, writhing in agony, the gun dropping from his hand.

It had all happened in a moment, and Chief Olowokere was already writhing in pain and coughing out blood on the laterite of the market place before the real meaning of his act dawned upon the people at the park and at the market place.

Then they cried out in terror and fled in all directions except in the direction where the body of Benjamin Benjamin lay still and where the body of Chief Olowokere lay not so still. One of the lorry touts, an admirer of Benjamin Benjamin, plump and short, cleared in one bound the four-foot fence round the park and pounded away down the road from the park and the market, shouting 'He has killed him! he has killed him!' Others followed his lead.

The arrival of Benjamin Benjamin at the lorry park that had earlier on attracted the crowd, had also attracted the police. Since the riots wherever and whenever two or three or more Ipaja men were gathered together, it was assumed that the spirit of lawlessness and disorder was within them.

So it was too, that in spite of their smart blue uniform, the whistles, the batons and all the other symbols of authority, the four police constables revealed that keepers of the King's peace were themselves subject to the ordinary failings of men. The same thing that had dispersed the men from the lorry park and the market place made the police constables flee from the scene of the double tragedy. But at least they fled in the same direction.

Then, amidst all the confusion, Josiah Olaiya came back.

The vicar of St John's kept a strange silence about his remarkable disappearance. He was most uncommunicative about the details of his experience in those forty-three days. Was he in Ipaja, locked up in someone's house? Was he in a village in the district, chained down to a tree stump like a goat? Was he in the grove of the Oro Cult, somewhere in the depth of the Igbodudu? Who for instance shaved his head bald? The vicar's hair was all gone, and his head was now shining bald, except for his wild, luxuriant beard.

When Olaiya was told of the murder of Benjamin Benjamin he became still less communicative about the missing forty-three days. No one could understand why, since relations between him and Benjamin Benjamin had been anything but friendly, the priest showed signs of regret that Benjamin Benjamin had died.

Udo Akpan called on Olaiya in his simple study in the church parsonage. Olaiya talked freely of the new church building and how he hoped that with the new cure for the cocoa disease, prosperity would again come to the land and how once again his congregation would remember in their rejoicings the Giver of all good gifts. He talked of the church school of which he was once headmaster and now manager, and hoped Udo Akpan would use his influence to get the school Government assistance. He talked of the falling standard in English Grammar and Composition taught in schools. He sighed for the good old days when he was himself a schoolteacher. That was a time when schoolteachers went about their work with dedication.

Udo Akpan was all eagerness when Olaiya disclosed that at the suggestion of the man who appeared to be their leader the people who took him away did not torture him at all.

On the contrary they treated him well and gave him the respect befitting a clergyman. But as suddenly as he had mentioned the subject the vicar of St John's dropped it and began to speak of other things, much to the disappointment of his guest. Much as Udo tried to bring him back to the subject of the curious disappearance Josiah Olaiya kept closed the window on this strange episode of his life.

In the hospital ward at Apeno Rev. Josiah Olaiya was shown to the bedside of Chief Olowokere the Obanla of Ipaja.

'Sit down, Pastor, sit down,' he said weakly.

'I am distressed to hear of all this tragedy, Chief. . . . The handwork of the devil. That is what it is.'

'I shot him and killed him,' the patient said weakly, staring into space. 'And I do not regret killing Benja-Benja. He was a crook. He ought to have been sent to jail for seven years for the amount of money he stole from the various amounts collected from the people. . . .

'Then he double-crossed me. First he ganged up with that bastard Joel who calls himself my father's son. All Ipaja knows that his mother was already made pregnant by an Apeno man before she ran back to my father! Benja-Benja conspired with Joel – and led the gang that destroyed my house. In spite of all I did to help him – Benja-Benja destroyed my house. . . .

'But Pastor, do you know that before that Benja-Benja had been making love to my second wife, the Apeno woman who was originally married to the Apeno Court Clerk! Remember the amount of fine I had to pay in respect of that shameless woman. To think that all the time that Benja-Benja was coming to my house he was coming not to see me but to see his mistress. . . .

'I shot him, and killed him. And do you know something, Pastor, I do not regret it. Let the Government do whatever they like with me.'

The vicar looked at the sick man intently. Tears welled up in his eyes as he said: 'May the Lord give you strength to love the memory of your dead neighbour as yourself. May the Lord give you strength to forgive those that trespass against you that He may in turn forgive you your own trespasses.'

For the murder of Benjamin Benjamin the Supreme Court in the capital city sentenced Chief Abraham Olowokere the Obanla of Ipaja to be hanged.

'I knew the law would catch up with Olowo some day,' Stanfield said to Udo Akpan when the news of Olowo's conviction reached Ipaja. He offered his cigarette case to Akpan. The latter selected a cigarette and muttered his thanks. 'I have known all along the fellow was a cheat.' He took a cigarette himself and held out a light for Akpan.

'You have known that all along, sir?' Udo asked, reflectively.

'Of course I have. What I did not know however, was that his neck was material for the hangman's rope. Pity he'd come to such a tragic end. . . . Still, I hear his lawyer has given notice of appeal.'

'You mean his lawyers. Seven of them. And that means waiting for another eighteen months or two years before the Supreme Court and later the Privy Council in London decide whether or not he shall be hanged.'

'We must give the accused person every chance to prove his innocence. It's the cardinal principle of our criminal law, Udo.'

'I know it is,' Udo said bitterly. 'Every accused person is deemed innocent till his guilt is proved . . . the onus of proof of guilt resting with the prosecution, and all that. I know it – and I know where it is leading this country.'

'Surely you can't hold that against our judicial system,' Stanfield said, taken aback. 'It is one of the best in the world. It is the one thing that the world will remember about the British.' He crushed his cigarette end in the ashtray.

'The British sense of justice and fair play! We applied it and assumed Benjamin Benjamin was innocent till his guilt was proved. . . . It was proved that he and his gang collected various sums of money from innocent men and women and that they put the money to improper use. . . . The Judge did not say that he disbelieved all this. He expressed his utter condemnation of Benjamin Benjamin. . . . But in spite of what His Worship believed and in spite of His Worship's condemnation of Benjamin Benjamin, His Worship discharged and acquitted him. The net result of His Worship's action? Benjamin Benjamin was once more let loose on both the innocent, trusting people of Ipaja – and on the Administration. That was British sense of justice and fair play.'

'Another cigarette, Udo?'

He took one. He knew he had spoken with some heat. He had learnt he could express himself freely before this older man who took more than passing interest in his career.

'You see, Udo, there was some technical point on which Benjamin Benjamin was let off. Something to do with the police charging him under the wrong section of the law. What could the judge do in the circumstances? Nothing? Till we can improve the police and the staff of the Attorney-General's office, these accidents will continue to occur.'

'But these are very expensive accidents, sir. That is the trouble. . . . Because of these accidents, and because of your sense of fair play and justice, a ruffian and spiv held the whole of the Administration to ransom. He held us to ranson for what might have been a long, long time.'

'Yes, until his own colleague mercifully intervened and put paid to his career!' He lit his third cigarette.

They both smoked in silence for a while. Udo was the first to speak. His face showed immediately that he had thought of another point. He said: 'Before you came to this country with Pax Britannica, a citizen of proved anti-community activities like Benjamin Benjamin was easily disposed of. He just vanished . . . After we in the Administration had failed to rid ourselves of the curse that was Benjamin Benjamin, an Ipaja man who had not heard of British sense of fair play and justice and in any case had no use for it got rid of the common enemy. He did it in a moment. We had failed to do it in two years.'

He stopped. Stanfield looked at him expectantly. Then Udo continued: 'After Olowo had shot his enemy he did not want to live. He turned his own gun on himself. But we did not allow him to die. We took him to the hospital, cut open his neck and removed the bullet. We sewed him up and are now nursing him back to health. In all that time we concentrated on him the best medical attention in the country. And after all this care and attention what do we do with Olowo? We are going to hang him by the neck till he be dead!'

CHAPTER TWENTY-EIGHT

Eighteen months passed.

Udo Akpan was putting the finishing touches to his Handing Over Notes. He had now completed his first tour as District Officer in the Ipaja–Apeno District and was due to start his leave in a few days. He was looking forward to it as he was to spend most of it in England attending a six weeks' conference on African administration in Oxford. He wrote:

With the death of Benjamin Benjamin, the conviction of Chief Abraham Olowokere for murder and the conviction of the men accused in the Ipaja Riots, the Igbodudu Land Appeal and other associated matters, must now be considered closed. (It should be mentioned that a letter from the office of the Attorney General on the subject of whether or not action could be instituted against Benjamin Benjamin for failing to appear before my Commission of Inquiry arrived in my office only a few weeks ago.) You should read Confidential File C.237/8 (3 volumes) for the history of Mr Benjamin Benjamin's activities in this District and of my Commission of Inquiry. You should read Confidential File 238/1 for a copy of the Court's proceedings and the judgement. . . . It is to be noted that even though the Privy Council has turned down Chief Abraham Olowokere's appeal, his lawyers have appealed to the Governor's Council for mercy. . . .

The construction of the Ipaja–Apeno water scheme is well under way (File 1765). Both town supplies are from the same source, the Agbara River, which flows all the year round. The Provincial Engineer told me that the job is being handicapped by the non-delivery of pipes from England. His headquarters has cabled Crown Agents about this and it is believed that the mail-boat sailing from Liverpool this week carries a good consignment of pipes. Efforts must be made by all concerned to consolidate the ground already won by the Administrator in bringing the Apenos and the Ipajas together since the unhappy days of Mr Benjamin Benjamin, and the present feeling of cooperation must not be allowed to flag due to any slowing down in the construction of the water supplies in the two towns. . . .

The plans of the Agricultural Department for the Igbodudu Farm Project are well advanced. You should read the memorandum from the Assistant Director of Agriculture, which was laid before the Legislative Council during the last session (File 296/1). There is to be a 16-acre cocoa nursery from which seedlings of the disease-resisting Brazilian strain are to be distributed at subsidized prices to farmers in the Apeno–Ipaja District. There will be a 320 acre pilot citrus farm and a 320 demonstration farm for cash crops. The joint Apeno–Ipaja Cooperative Farmers' Union are very keen on the project and efforts must be made to see that their enthusiasm is sustained. . . .

Udo Akpan's successor was another African. A few years older than Udo, he possessed the additional advantage of being a member of the major tribe of which the Apenos and the Ipajas were sub-tribes. He was one of four recent appointments made on the recommendation of Stanfield, now Acting Deputy Commissioner for the Protectorate, that, as a result of Udo Akpan's success in the particularly difficult circumstances in the Ipaja–Apeno District, more Africans be appointed to the Administrative Service in continuation of the experiment.

'Apparently you were in London at the same time that I was in Cambridge,' Udo said as they sat down together in the office, the junior man glancing through the Handing Over Notes file. They had just come back from a visit to the Oba of Ipaja during which Udo Akpan introduced his successor to the old man. 'I wonder we did not meet in London. I used to spend most of my holidays in London.'

'I suppose you stayed at the Colonial Students' Hostel at Earls Court. I certainly remember having seen you at one of the meetings at Student Movement House, at Gower Street. At a lecture given by the Secretary of State for the Colonies —'

'An account of our Stewardship in our Overseas Territories". I remember quite well how the students heckled the old man so much that he was nearly in tears.'

'I have seen the boys actually break up a similar meeting. At Conway Hall. Called by the Fabian Society. The boys were just impossible. The chairman had to call for order several times. Most disgraceful incident – I was quite ashamed of the performance of our students at that meeting. Mark you, most of what the old man was saying was typical British rot. You know the usual British attitude of the wonderful speed at which they were moving in the Colonies. How, if they kept that speed, the countries of West Africa might become independent territories in the lifetime of some Englishmen in that audience. . . . Difficult to remove their mind from that set groove. They think in terms of centuries instead of decades and years. . . . And what do you think of the old Oba?' Udo Akpan came back to earth to the live subject of Apeno–Ipaja administration. 'You will find the old man a completely sober man. He'd been scared by the way the end came to Benjamin Benjamin. And by the fate of Chief Olowokere. A great advantage you speak the old man's language. I envy you.'

'A grand old man. Reminds me of the Oba of my own hometown. I very much hope he'll not take advantage of my speaking his language.'

'Of course it works both ways,' Udo said reflectively. 'An advantage nevertheless. . . .'

They were both silent for some time. Udo smoked, while his companion made some note on the cover of a file. Then Udo spoke: 'By the way, I told you yesterday I'd tell you more of the Rev. Olaiya's strange disappearance.'

'Oh yes, what really happened to him?'

'He himself wouldn't tell a soul about it. But we've now got pretty well the essentials of the story. He was kidnapped by the Oro Cult Secret Society and taken to their grove. Two things are peculiar about the kidnapping. He was taken to a grove outside Ipaja District; also he was well treated. In fact it appears that rather than a punishment the kidnapping was apparently designed to give the holy man a course of instruction on the origins of the tribe and its early government. The whole thing has affected his outlook profoundly. He was made to swear to secrecy before they showed him anything. That's why he keeps sealed lips. You can't get anything out of him.'

'How interesting.'

'Most interesting. You being a son of the soil, as it were, you may find it worth your while to join the Secret Society. You may well find that the Apajas of old may have a thing or two to teach us about administration. Cigarette?'

'Oh, I should tell you something about the file on post-mortems,' Udo Akpan said after some time, picking the file in question. 'You will find it voluminous. The police keep on writing all sorts of letters about the cause of this accident or that accident. The accident probably occurred so long ago that no one even remembers which body was involved in which accident.'

'Oh yes. And the D.O. comes into all this?'

'Very much so, I'm afraid. The necessity for post-mortems is one of those things which in my opinion require re-examination in the peculiar circumstances of African administration. A man is run over . . . by a lorry. Several other people see the lorry crush him. Death is instantaneous. Yet the hard-pressed doctor, with a long queue of dying patients waiting for medical attention spends his literally precious time cutting up the corpse of the accident victim.'

He stopped for a moment, lighting another cigarette before he continued. His companion said nothing, though he indicated that he was following Udo with interest.

'After he's toyed with a few organs he sews up the blessed thing again. He then writes in his medical language a report on the cause of death. Of course the scores of men and women who saw the accident – the lorry and the victim – knew the cause of death. It did not require an M.B., Ch.B. to put two and two together after hearing the crash and seeing the lorry and the mangled body of the victim.'

'Awful,' said the other. 'Sounds quite senseless in the circumstances. Suppose the police insist on it?'

'Yes, the law insists on it. Something to do with possible litigation arising out of the accident. . . . I have always believed that it is a crime to leave the living dying while we waste precious time toying with the dead in these circumstances. Difficult to blame the ordinary folk who see some sinister motive in the whole thing. You'll remember too the great sanctity with which the African holds the corpse of a dead relative.'

The African doctor from the Government hospital came in at that moment. The two Administrative officers laughed at the coincidence. 'You two talking politics?' the doctor asked mischievously, sitting familiarly at the edge of Udo's desk. 'You must remember your General Orders.'

'Strangely enough we were discussing the all-important subject of post-mortems,' Udo explained.

'For God's sake think of something else to discuss, not post-mortems,' the doctor said in disgust. 'Anything else. The disqualification of Civil servants from politics, for instance.'

'Yes,' Udo sighed. 'We are all disqualified by the General Orders from discussing publicly our national affairs. General Orders – this bible of the Civil Service was written by expatriates who had the British Public Service at the back of their mind. In Britain the civil servant does not engage in politics.'

'Does he have to anyway?' the doctor asked.

'That's just the point,' Udo continued. 'The British Civil Servant does not have to engage in politics because there are literally hundreds of thousands of fellow Britons who are outside the Civil Service and who are available to engage in politics both at the national and at the local government levels. The civil servant can therefore sit at his desk to carry out his own assignment, that of implementing policy decisions.'

He paused for a moment to collect his thoughts. 'But here in this country the situation is sadly different. The best brains of the country are with a few exceptions all in the Civil Service. Can this country with its limited resources in educated man-power afford to have their mouths padlocked in the Civil Service while second-rate and sometimes semi-literate men are saddled with the very important duty of legislating and taking executive decisions for the State? Can we not have a state of affairs where the civil servant can makes his views known publicly on matters on which he is by qualification and experience competent to express views?'

'Absolute nonsense, that's what I think the whole thing is,' the doctor said. 'Udo, I think you should start writing new General Orders for our independence. We must look into the possibility of the civil servant having sufficient freedom to make constructive contributions to matters of public interest without such freedom developing into license for engaging in irresponsible activities.'

'And Udo, what's this I heard about the lawyer charging the Ipaja people six thousand pounds for the Igbodudu land case?' asked the doctor, perplexed.

'No, not six thousand,' Udo said, mischief lighting up his face. 'He charged the very modest fee of four thousand two hundred pounds.'

'Four thousand two hundred,' echoed the doctor.

Udo continued. 'The evidence of the expert from the Land Department was that the market value of the land was only one thousand six hundred and eighty pounds.'

'So that if the Ipaja people had won the case against the Apenos they would have spent four thousand and two hundred pounds and incurred some other expenses to get back land that was worth only under two thousand,' the doctor said, knocking the ash off his cigarette.

'It's ridiculous,' the new District Officer observed.

'I am the last to hold to ridicule the learned profession,' Udo continued. They all laughed. 'However, I'll say as an

African that the time has come that the African lawyers in our midst should think of themselves first as Africans and only next as lawyers. It is my view that the sacred objective of building a new nation cannot be achieved unless our lawyers – and indeed all our professional men – exercise a new kind of restraint.'

'I can't agree with you more,' said the doctor.

'Look at what these lawyers do in the courts,' Udo went on. 'Taking advantage of the inefficiency and corruption of the police, the ignorance of the masses and the woefully inadequate number of Crown Counsels, to handle criminal cases to the advantage of individuals who embezzle public funds and enrich themselves at the expense of the public. This is nothing short of a crime against a new nation. That's what I think. Democracy's a wonderful thing. I have the greatest respect for a legal system which gives the individual the benefit of the doubt in a society where the State Attorney and the officers of the peace are adequate and alive to their responsibilities.'

'Tell me more about Benjamin Benjamin,' the doctor said. 'You know I hadn't arrived from England when he operated in this area. From what one hears at the Club he must have been a character.'

'Benjamin Benjamin, of blessed memory,' sighed Udo in reminiscence. 'You know every time I saw him he reminded me of a chap that used to pull great crowds at Hyde Park in London. A chap from Central Africa. . . . I used to frequent Hyde Park to listen to him, and to the others like him. You see the fellow fitted in very well in the pattern of British concept of democracy and the freedom of the individual to say what he likes. . . . You know they provide the Irish revolutionary and the London blackshirt with police escort when they are making their bitter and sometimes personal attacks on the British King and Government, to protect them from possible physical attack from the more loyal members of the audience. . . . Benjamin Benjamin in Hyde Park would be a most interesting fellow. No one would take him seriously.

No more seriously than they take a clown at the Circus. His black face would be a source of amusement to a good number of ice-cream eating Yorkshire housewives holidaying down in London. And all the nonsense he had to say would pale into insignificance compared with the many million words of greater nonsense that several generations of greater wretches and cranks than himself have said before him to several generations of audiences. He would be completely harmless in the London context. . . . But it is an entirely different thing in this country where the masses, illiterate and ignorant, believe everything that anyone that can read and write tells them.'

'Hear, hear,' the doctor cried again in enthusiasm. 'That's the point. You've got it Udo.'

'Benjamin Benjamin's three and a half years' operations in Ipaja have shown conclusively that whatever brand of democracy we import into this country we must make sure that we sift out the seed of the disease that will otherwise choke to death the new freedom from imperialism which we hope to achieve soon.'

'There is one thing that worries me about the Benjamin Benjamins in our midst,' the other administrative officer said seriously. 'You see, the ordinary folk cannot easily distinguish the half-educated and the spiv from the honest educated individual like ourselves. To the old Oba and people of Ipaja Benjamin Benjamin and you Udo Akpan belonged to the same class – the class of those who can read and write and speak the White Man's language. And when the ordinary folk discover the dishonesty and worthlessness of the Benjamin Benjamins, to them it is not only the Benjamin Benjamins that have failed but all of us who belong to the same class of those that can read and write and speak the White Man's language. And when the Oba and his people begin to distrust us, my God, it will take a long time before we can win back their confidence.'

'A long time indeed,' agreed the doctor.

'And these particular collections raise the much bigger issue of public collections. The principle of making collections for carrying out community development schemes is most admirable and praiseworthy. I am myself the product of such a scheme. Without the self-sacrifice of the many thousand men and women of my community who contributed their pounds and shillings and pence my higher education in Britain would have been impossible. But the unfortunate point is that the overheads in these collections are very high, even when there isn't a Benjamin Benjamin around to misappropriate the funds.'

'How do you mean?' said the doctor.

'What do the people do? A town decide they want to build a community school. A team of five patriots sets out from that town with a fanfare on a tour of a remote district in the country where a few of their fellow-townsmen are scattered in remote villages. Their townsmen receive them cordially, and entertain them lavishly. Then they give to them for the fund what little they can afford after the expenses of entertaining their guests. Five shillings, ten shillings, sometimes a pound. Very seldom over that. But the point is that the fellow who pays ten shillings to the fund reckons that he has paid not ten shillings but twenty or twenty-five, because entertaining the chaps from home has cost him an extra ten or fifteen shillings.'

'Too true, man.'

'And what is still more sad about the whole thing is this: after the train fares and other overhead expenses of the chaps from home have been deducted from their collection, only a fraction of two or three shillings of the chap's original donation ever gets added to the amount of money that is actually spent on building a new school To my mind this willingness on the part of the communities to contribute themselves to much-needed services is something that we must preserve in our national character. But how can we make the whole thing operate with efficiency? How?'